COCKSUCKER

LUCAS MILLIRON

GRINDHOUSE
PRESS

For my dad.

Without your stories about Bigfoot and Skunk Apes, your love of horror, and macabre sense of humor, not only would this book not be here, but neither would I.

Other titles by Lucas Milliron

Tim E. Less
Becoming Series
Away from Home

Collections
Prismatic Words

1

ABIGAIL COULD TASTE THE BLOOD on her brother's foreskin.

"Clive!" she hollered. "What the fuck? You said you showered!"

"Yesterday," Clive replied.

"You forget under your foreskin again? Why does your dick taste like blood?"

"Mama's on the rag."

"Motherfucker!"

"Frog face!"

"I'm tellin' Pa!"

"You know damn well he don't like no snitches."

"Fine. But you better nut quick this time. We still got chores."

Abigail dropped her purple, saggy, brown-stained panties and spread her legs. Her blond pubic hair stuck up and out like a frayed pile of hay and stank like the bog out back. She scooted her bare ass closer to him. The gritty, rusty bed of the old Ford Ranger itched the top of her crack.

Clive snorted deeply. He went to spit in his hand but didn't blow hard enough. The foamy white and green loogy slipped down his lip and chin like a raw egg yolk. Abigail burst out laughing, pointing at her brother as his cock began to wilt in his rough, dry hand.

"Motherfucker can't even spit right!"

"Fuck you!"

"Not with that dead ass snail you ain't."

Clive examined his penis. His ball sack hung low, his flaccid penis draped over it. It kind of did look like a dead yellow and pink snail. Clive's nose whistled as he giggled.

"It does look like a dead snail, don't it?" Clive laughed again.

Abigail rolled her eyes. Clive made sure he didn't miss his palm and spat into his hand. He rubbed the slimy substance along the shaft of his snail meat. It swelled, and Abigail fell back on the truck bed and reared her hips toward him again. Clive trembled as his cock slid inside. He grunted like a pig, thrusting his hips back and forth. Abigail yawned as she dug at the dirt under her nails. Clive's face dripped with sweat that splashed across Abigail's shirt.

"You gonna say anything?" Clive grumbled.

"Like what?" Abigail asked, annoyed.

"I don't care! Say somethin' nice!"

"Oh baby, your snail meat is so thick."

"Bitch!"

Abigail feigned excitement and pleasure. Clive's body vibrated, and his legs threatened to buckle. He pulled out his throbbing member and expelled sticky white and yellow semen across her pelvis. He grunted and whooped wildly, shaking his head like a dog in dirt. He spun his penis in the air like a helicopter, sending droplets of cum across his sister's shirt and face.

"Cut that shit out!" she yelled.

"Looks like the sugar glaze on one of them little ol' honey

buns!" Clive laughed.

Abigail cleaned off the cum with her dirty panties the best she could.

"Where you goin'?" Clive asked.

"To feed the damn chickens!" she yelled as she got back on her feet. "I told you, we gots chores to do."

"Aw hell," Clive exhaled, trying to catch his breath.

Abigail threw her long hair over her shoulders and went on to do her chores. Clive pulled up his tattered jeans, carefully tucking his sticky, crusty snail to one side as he zipped up the front.

"Hey Clive!" Abigail shouted from the henhouse. "We got us a problem!"

"What now?" Clive hollered back.

"Get yer ass over here!"

Clive sucked his teeth and made his way to the henhouse. The gate was ripped from its hinges, tearing gashes in the two-by-four doorframe in the process. The coop was a mess of feathers and dead birds. They lay sprawled out across the dirt floor, their necks bent in unnatural angles with naked patches of feathers exposing three strange puncture wounds. Even stranger was how clean the bodies were; there was no blood, only a few drips around the puncture marks and surrounding feathers.

"What the hell can do that?" Abigail asked.

"Coyotes maybe," Clive said, crouching down to pick up one of the dead hens.

"Coyotes, my ass," Abigail sneered. "They'd have their guts strung up all in here like Christmas lights. All the good meat's still on the bone."

"Maybe a chicken hawk?"

"A chicken hawk just fell out the sky one day and ripped open this here cage Pa built?"

"It's just an idea! I ain't hear any of your stupid ideas."

"I betcha it was the skunk ape."

"No, Daddy went and set up some of them traps for Curious ol' Bob out there."

"I don't get why you gotta up and name everything you meet."

"'Cause it deserves a name! If it moves, scuttles, or makes noises, it deserves a name."

"Then why didn't you name the hens?"

"'Cause hens is for eatin'. I named the truck Big Jimmy."

"That damn piece of shit?"

"Don't call Big Jimmy a piece of shit!"

"Can you calm down and focus? We got a henhouse full of dead hens!"

"Think Mama gonna get mad?"

"Fuck yeah! *I'm* mad! I say we go out there and find that old skunk ape and show him."

"Pa ain't gonna like this none."

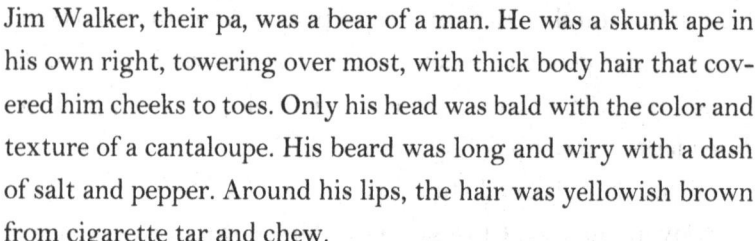

Jim Walker, their pa, was a bear of a man. He was a skunk ape in his own right, towering over most, with thick body hair that covered him cheeks to toes. Only his head was bald with the color and texture of a cantaloupe. His beard was long and wiry with a dash of salt and pepper. Around his lips, the hair was yellowish brown from cigarette tar and chew.

The family lived in a two-bedroom manufactured home. It was old as dirt with parquet floors and wood paneling throughout. The kitchen was wallpapered with a floral print that was tacky even when it was first put in. After years of cooking, grease fires, and cigarette smoke, the colors had faded to a sickly brown and green, flaking like snakeskin from humid Florida summers.

Jim spent most of his days hunting for squirrel and deer for the

Red Crab, a quaint restaurant in the middle of nowhere along alligator alley owned by him and his wife. She made the best fried frog legs in all of the Everglades. His wife, Margay, was a pear. She was a sweet, bell-shaped woman who would go out of her way to make anyone comfortable. Margay was a perfect hostess for the Red Crab.

The Red Crab was a staple in southern Florida. It was a big blue building originally built in 1902 on stilts to keep it dry in the rainy season, and though there was no air conditioning, the large screen windows, patios, and doors were placed just right to catch every breeze that blew by and keep out the mosquitoes. The inside was traditional Florida cracker construction.

Oak benches and booths covered the pinewood floors. The tables were a mishmash of whatever they'd found driving around suburbia on garbage day. Everything they took got a good washing and was mended with rough nails, glue, and a healthy amount of duct tape. The ceiling was a latticework of exposed beams.

At one point, Jim's father got the idea of tying lanterns to the rafters to make the lighting more romantic. It worked great for about a night, at least until the string caught fire and nearly burned the roof right off the building. Most of the badly burned pieces were replaced, but in several places much of the wood was still heavily charred. He left the lanterns hanging throughout the restaurant – too much work to take them all down. In empty patches where the fire burned everything, Jim hung beer bottles by string to give some weird kind of continuity to the decor.

The children were left to decorate the bathrooms. The men's room was wallpapered with clips of naked women from nudie books Jim used to collect. Most of the sink and mirror were plastered with pictures of bushy pubes and beaver hunt specials. Clive was especially fond of hairy women. The women's room was decorated in a similar fashion, only less overt and more suggestive. Cowboys and Indians were the primary theme, with muscular men hiding their vegetables in provocative and suggestive ways. Some men used machete-sized Bowie knives, hats, and thickly knotted ropes to suggest the man's endowment.

The kitchen was a shack built in the late seventies by Jim's father when his family bought the property for less than eight hundred dollars. It was kept away from the main building to keep the dining rooms cooler and to hide the secret ingredients to Margay's stews. Her secret meat pies were such a delight, a few local city boys came in on a regular basis to take home two or three at a time. They always asked what it was and made wild guesses like duck, pork, or lamb. But Margay always smiled at them kindly and proclaimed love was the only secret ingredient. There's nothing wrong with eating squirrel or possum, but the city folk don't take kindly to such exotic protein.

By and large, their signature dishes were the frog legs and blue crab sandwiches. Both the crabs and frogs were hand-battered and fried in lard, the way Jim's mama used to make when he was a child. She passed the recipe to his wife before she died, God rest her soul. The legs required the most care. The breadcrumbs were scratch made, and the frogs fresh from the glades. They needed to be just the right size, not too thin or the meat would cook too fast, and not too fat or the meat would fry too long and turn greasy.

It was a family business. Jim's number one rule, above all else, was take the city folks' money and keep the secrets in the family.

◄─────────────────►

Jim came home late that afternoon just as the humid day came to a close. He managed to get a large potato sack full of squirrels and five fat possums under his right arm, and in his left hand, he dragged a four-foot alligator. Jim carried his catch like a great swamp Santa Claus. He wore a white tank top with yellow stains under the arms and pink splotches across the front from old hunting kills and field dressing in the Everglades. He smiled with a wooden pipe he'd made two weeks earlier pinched between his lips. He'd done real good.

"Margay!" he hollered from the yard as he came up to the back door. "We got good eats tonight!"

"Jim," Margay said, her voice shrill and tired as she came into the yard. "We got some problems with the henhouse."

Jim looked like a child ready to show off his macaroni art only to be scolded for using the last of the macaroni.

"What you mean a problem in the henhouse?" he asked.

"Put that on the counter and just head over to the chicken coop," Margay ordered.

Jim did as he was told and went to the henhouse just out of sight from the restaurant. Clive's truck was still parked around back near the barn. Abigail stood by the broken henhouse with her hands on her hips. Jim remembered when Margay used to give him that look back when she was younger. The thought swelled in his crotch. Jim turned his attention back to the chickens. The henhouse was a mess of feathers and dead hens.

"What the damn hell?" Jim said, resting his massive palm on the broken doorframe.

"We got no ideas." Abigail shrugged.

"Where's your brother?" Jim asked.

"Usin' the john." Abigail pointed to the outhouse a few yards back.

Jim grimaced and stormed toward the shitter.

"Get your ass out here, boy!" Jim growled.

"Yes, Pa!" Clive scuffled inside the outhouse, shaking the wood panels as he stumbled out the broken door.

Jim looked at his son. Clive was a thin young man with leather-colored arms and a face scarred from bad acne. The boy looked like someone tried to put out a fire with a pitchfork. Kid couldn't track, couldn't shoot, couldn't spit, and couldn't work much without bitching and complaining. Jim wasn't even sure the squat was his. Too much of his mother's side in him. But Jim was stuck with him until he turned eighteen. At least that's what the law said the last time he tried to kick him out at twelve years old.

Jim looked at a chicken with a broken neck. Its head slumped over the edge of the roost like a wilted celery stick. He picked up the hen and felt its body. It was lighter than he expected. Along its neck, he saw the three puncture marks and found little drops of blood spattered amongst the feathers. Whatever killed them, sucked out all the blood.

"Grab yer gun," Jim said.

"What're we gonna do?" Clive asked.

"We fixin' to find whatever done this," Jim answered. "You ain't no good at shootin', but whatever done this don't know that. Maybe you'll get lucky and show me wrong."

Clive looked at his Pa. He hadn't done anything right in the man's eyes since the day he was born. Maybe this was his chance to show him wrong. Clive stuffed a set of zip ties and the camp knife he'd been using to help fix the henhouse in his pocket, breathed in deep, and ran out to grab his gun.

"You sure about this?" Margay asked. "It's gettin' dark soon and the restaurant's about to open for supper. You should rest your head, get some food in ya, and set out in the morning."

"Whatever done this is a monster," Jim replied.

"Think it was Curious ol' Bob?"

"Nah. What done this was somethin' else. I've seen this before."

"What is it?"

"Back in '88. Somethin' came out of the swamp, somethin' evil. It slaughtered all the chickens, bled 'em dry as raisins. Margay, we got ourselves a cocksucker."

2

THE EASY MEALS DROVE HER closer and closer to people, an idea she didn't like until she'd discovered a taste for hens. She could still taste the chicken's sticky, sweet blood on her lips. The brown hens were her favorite. They tasted like sweet corn. If only their tiny bodies carried more than a few delicious sips, she might not need to hide out near people so often.

She could smell the humans from miles away. They carried a strange, fatty odor, pungent with the scent of fake flowers and musk that burned her nose and stung the back of her palate. Humans always stank of their cities. Usually they tasted like gristle and seawater. Their presence, however, meant other smaller, tastier treats would follow. Birds, squirrels, possums, and raccoons were just a few. The ones she liked the most were the animals they kept for themselves—their hens, goats, cows, and dogs.

After breaking into the henhouse and eating her fill, she fled back into the Everglades. Not long after, a smell ran across her nose. It was sharp, smoky, sweet, and briny. It smelled like fire and burning meat. She followed it, crouching on all fours, and waited in the brush.

There were few things Michael loved more than craft beer and beards, his vintage teardrop camper, flannel shirts, and his girl-friend, Jessica. The two of them loved nature even more. They basked in the great outdoors, drinking in all the fresh air and sun-shine they could.

Florida was especially hot in the summer, so Michael rocked his salmon-colored shorts in front of the grill in his light blue, short-sleeve shirt. He dipped his phone in his pocket for only a few seconds before pulling it out again to read and reread the burger recipe and instructions he'd found online. He made sure to use only the best organic grass-fed beef, free from antibiotics and GMOs. The recipe was always gluten free, as Jessica experienced a strange, emotional reaction whenever she ate wheat gluten.

She once ate a Caesar salad, but a single crouton was more than enough to contaminate the dish. Jessica claimed the rest was a blur, but Michael distinctly remembered the way she cried while pinning him down with a knife at his throat. He loved her dearly but could have done without the manic episodes.

Jessica didn't need prescription glasses. In fact, she'd even popped the lenses out after buying them from the eyeglass store. As a result, the oversized aviators draped over her face like socks on a rooster. She'd worn her skin-tight, striped tank top and high-waisted denim shorts, which proved very helpful in the hot after-noon humidity, aside from the chafing.

Jessica sat cross-legged in the folding chair, swirling her glass of merlot as she watched Michael fling his meat on the grill. Maybe it was the heat or, perhaps, the wine, but there was some-thing about a man hunched over something as primal as fire that made her insides somersault. She slipped her feet into her Birkenstock sandals on the ground in front of her and moseyed over to Michael, too tied up in grilling to notice her.

Michael jumped in surprise as Jessica wrapped her arms around him, the wine glass still in her hand.

"Would ya mind passing me an IPA from the cooler?" He laughed, flipping the meat as one side gently cooked to perfection.

"In a minute," Jessica giggled, her fingers tracing the outline of the growing bulge in his pants.

"I don't wanna burn the burgers." Michael tried to maintain composure in front of the grill.

"It'll only be a minute." Jessica kissed the side of his neck and nibbled his ear.

As much as Michael hated wasting food, more primal, desperate urges throbbed inside his pants. Jessica had loved many men, savoring their different cultures like fine dining. Michael wasn't the most well-endowed man she'd ever given herself to, but something about his charm and attentive nature to her needs more than his own made up for both his length and girth. Besides, five inches was average for a white American male.

Michael abandoned the burgers and lifted Jessica into the air. Gingerly, he walked her over toward his Volvo 240 wagon and set her down on the hood of the car. They kissed, their lips tasting and feeling each other, breathing as one living body. Jessica imagined him ripping off her clothes and ravaging her body like she was a sex worker. Michael thought of the wine on her lips and wondered if it'd stain his teeth.

The two worked diligently at undressing themselves, their mouths locked as if separating them meant suffocation. Neither noticed the creature stalking them from the woods not ten feet away. It skulked low to the ground, its dark, wrinkled skin blending in with the shadows.

$$\longleftrightarrow$$

She watched the two rutting on top of the car. Their musky smells of genital juices blended with the sweet meats charring over the fire into a tantalizing perfume. She tasted the air with her long forked tongue, savoring their scent and flavor. They were salty and fatty, a wash of rich umami flavors. Most importantly, they were fat with blood.

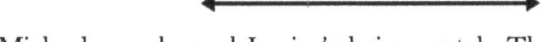

Michael raw dogged Jessica's hairy snatch. Their pubes knotted with pink, slimy vaginal juice and pre-cum. It smelled like sex as wild as the Everglades in which they fucked. Michael ran his thumb along Jessica's engorged clit, hunching over as he tried to lick her lemon-sized breasts while maintaining rhythm.

It was a complicated dance he'd perfected in the bedroom but found increasingly difficult on the hot metal hood. The couple were sweating long before they'd started fucking, but it rained down Michael's face and dripped down his nose and beard while he grunted like a stalled lawn mower.

Long talons ripped into his back. He cried out as the pain yanked him from near climax into a world of agony. Confused and on the edge of orgasm, he ejaculated as his hard cock slipped from Jessica's dripping cunt. They screamed together in a chorus of horror as the creature struck again. It bit him in the leg, its three needle-like fangs sinking deep into his calf muscle.

Jessica climbed higher onto the car, watching helplessly as her boyfriend was mauled by some terrible creature. Michael fell and was soon overtaken by the monster. It was over in seconds as the thing bit down hard on his neck from behind, making him shake violently. His neck snapped, and he was dead.

She might have let the woman go, might have been satisfied with the man she'd taken down so easily, but instead the woman wanted to play. The woman did as all prey does—she ran. So, she chased. The woman was slow and cumbersome as she ran, mostly naked, through the brush. The pine trees and palm fronds poked and sliced her exposed flesh, causing her to fall more than once. She enjoyed the chase, the hunting of her prey. She allowed the woman to get back to her feet, to win by inches before knocking her down again.

She slashed the back of her ankle with her long claws. The woman fell, sobbing loudly as she leaked from her eyes and nose. She circled her prey, staying just out of sight in the dense foliage before climbing a tree right above her.

$$\longleftrightarrow$$

Jessica didn't want to die. She wanted to save Michael, but she was defenseless. The creature's nails slashed her Achilles tendon. The pain was excruciating, and standing was impossible. She crawled in the dirt carpeted in royal palm tree fronds and pine needles.

Heaving with loud, labored breaths, Jessica looked over her shoulder, expecting to see the monster bearing down on top of her. To her surprise, there was nothing there. She gritted her teeth and grunted, willing herself to survive, to live, to keep fucking running.

Something in the trees rustled above her. Jessica stopped, that fatal curiosity breathing down her neck. She looked up and saw the silhouette of the thing scurrying through the trees. Before she had time to scream, it pounced.

Jessica could feel its long needle-like teeth scraping against the bones in her neck as its powerful jaws crushed her windpipe. She gasped for a breath that would not come, choking as the creature punctured her jugular. Blood spilled from her wounds as it released her. Her fingers stung like pins and needles, as did her toes and feet. Soon, a cold, numb sensation washed over her as the creature pressed its lips to her throat and suckled on her gaping wounds.

It didn't take long for her to remember why she hated hunting humans so much. The woman tasted salty and the blood bitter. It coated her tongue with a fatty film. Maybe it was the thrill of the chase or the work she'd put into hunting the woman down, but she was hungry, and no meal, no matter how unsavory, was to be wasted.

3

FREDDY COULD STILL TASTE THE bourbon on the man's lips. The world was spinning out of control. How could it be so hot and humid this late at night? He did the only thing that made sense; he took off his sweaty shirt. The older man explored his flesh with his hands and lips. Freddy's nipples hardened, as did the bulge in his pants. His head was filled with adrenaline, along with the smell of booze, sweat, and the stranger's cologne.

Freddy closed his eyes while the man's strong hands worked their way around his belt buckle. He could feel his body quiver as the man suckled his earlobe. Freddy fought the urge to moan, to cry out in rapture. He bit his lip, trying to stave off the intensity of this stranger's lust.

"Freddy," Winston said from behind them.

"Fuck . . ." Freddy opened his eyes.

His heart dropped, sobriety tight on its heels. Freddy didn't know how long he'd been watching, but it was long enough. Winston saw the silver-haired gentleman in a white button-up shirt and cream-colored skinny jeans with his hand in his boyfriend's pants. Not all the air in the world could quench his lungs' thirst.

Freddy squeezed his eyes shut, tears spilling across his cheeks.

"Stop," he said softly to the silver fox. "Please."

The man did as Freddy asked, rubbing his nose and straightening a few stray hairs with his palm. He found his composure. As he stepped out of the alleyway, he glanced at Winston as he walked by. Winston crossed his arms and looked back at Freddy, who'd slumped to the ground against the brick wall by the dumpster.

Freddy looked up at him. Winston was a marathon runner with dark umber skin as soft as purple calla lilies. He was sweating, beads dripping from his nose like fresh dew.

Winston looked down at Freddy. He wasn't the best-looking man, but when he cleaned up, he looked like a solid eight. Winston didn't mind his chunky belly, but in the darkness of the alley, the way the sweat glistened off his rolls looked slobbish and downright disgusting.

"You son of a bitch," Winston said, his eyes red and voice thick.

"I'm sorry," Freddy sniffled.

"You just fucking proposed to me!"

"And you said no!"

"I said I wasn't ready. Clearly, you weren't either."

"Winston. Please, I love you. I really do!"

"Then what the fuck was that? That man, that fucking stranger, had his hand in your goddamn pants!"

"I'm drunk."

"Lame excuse."

"Don't go! I wanna get through this, I want us to work this out."

"How can I?"

"I'm so sorry."

Winston was out of things to say. He turned around and left

Freddy in the alley. His mind raced, struggling to find something else to think about. The image of his lover kissing another man with his hand around his genitals was burned in his head. Lucky for Winston, Key West was full of places he could go to forget.

Fantasy Fest was in full swing. The streets were lined with pride flags, purple triangles, drag queens, and all manner of colorful queer folk. The night was swimming with music, booze, and glitter. People wore brightly colored leotards, clear high heels with LEDs, or nothing but thin layers of paint. It was the best night of their lives come to the worst ending imaginable. Freddy and Winston both wondered how things could get any worse.

Winston bumped into Jennifer and Dean at the Rum Runner. The small bedroom-size bar was cramped enough as it was, but with Freddy's sister and her boyfriend necking, it felt even tighter. As soon as he saw them, he turned around to leave.

Jennifer was a personal trainer and her curvaceous figure could bring scores of men to their knees. Freddy always joked she'd gotten her mother's Hispanic booty and their father's flat chest. That was until she had her first boob job. Her boyfriend, Dean, was a swarthy man. Though he'd been born with a silver spoon in his mouth, he kept himself in rugged shape with his CrossFit company. The flowing green dress Jennifer wore allowed for easy and discreet access to her more intimate areas, while Dean's attire only suited to accentuate his strong physique.

"Hey there!" Jen laughed. "What are you guys up to? Where's Freddy?"

"You might wanna look in the back alley," Winston said, still making his way out of the bar.

"What's wrong?" Jennifer quickly got up.

"Jen!" Dean exclaimed, falling as he went to lean on her and she wasn't there.

Winston was already halfway down the road by the time Jennifer caught up with him.

"What's going on?"

"I can't do this," Winston tried to explain, but sadness swallowed his words.

"Come here!" Jen pulled him close to her, hugging him as he sobbed loudly into her chest.

"What's going on?" Dean said as he finally reached them.

"I dunno." Jen shrugged her shoulders and asked Winston, "Did you guys have a fight?"

"Sorta." Winston tried to compose himself. "Freddy, he proposed to me. "

"Oh my God." Jen covered her mouth in surprise. "What did you say?"

"It's too soon! We've only been dating for six months. I know I'm his first boyfriend, but it's too soon."

"How'd he take it?"

"Bad enough to find himself an older man."

"He did what?" Jen's Latina switch flipped. "Where is he?"

Winston walked them around the corner. Freddy was right where he'd left him. Vomit covered his naked chest and unbuckled pants. He was crying, almost hysterical as he coughed, trying to catch his breath.

"*Puto!*" Jennifer shouted. "What the fuck is wrong with you?!"

Jennifer pulled off her flip-flop and began whaling on her younger brother.

"I'm sorry!" Freddy cried, shielding his face with his arms as best as his drunken muscles could.

"You bring this man on vacation with your family," she spat with rapid-fire aggression. "You propose to him, and just because you don't like his answer, you go and fucking cheat on him!

Pendejo! Don't you hold your arms up at me!"

"Honey!" Dean said, grabbing her arm. "Let's not make a scene!"

"This *estúpido* shouldn't have cheated then!"

"He's your brother."

"He's a stupid ass!"

"We still have the whole vacation ahead of us!"

"Leave him! He doesn't deserve it!"

"We already paid for this trip! We've got hotel accommodations, a rental car, and plane tickets. He's your brother, for God's sake!"

"He ain't my brother. Our Ma never raised us that way. I don't know where he got that shit from."

"Sweetheart, please, stop yelling for five seconds!"

"You think I'm yelling? You think *this* is yelling? Oh, I'm gonna show you. *Pinche puto* get the fuck up! We're taking you to the airport and flying your ass back to California! And we ain't got no time for showers neither."

"Stop!" Winston shouted. "Stop! Please. This isn't what I wanted. Look, he's a shithead, but I don't want to ruin this vacation for everyone else. I can pay for my own flight back."

"Will everyone calm the hell down!" Dean yelled. "Listen, we prepaid this road trip months ago. There's a campsite we're going to just north of Miami. Let's make it that far and we'll discuss it from there. I think everyone is a little frustrated, a little drunk, and we need to sober up. Let's at least have a day or two before we make any decisions."

"Okay," Freddy said, still crying on the floor.

"Okay?" Dean said, letting go of Jen's arm.

"Fine," she sneered.

Dean gave Winston a stern look.

"Sure." Winston nodded his head.

"All right then," Dean said, sighing with relief. "Let's get your brother to the motel. Get him showered and into bed. The hangover he's gonna wake up with is punishment enough. And put your shoe back on!"

4

THE EVERGLADES IS A RIVER of grass. Sawgrass and cattails line the narrow banks as far as the eye can see, with only a few mangrove forests peppering the horizon. Regular boats can get bogged down in its shallow waters, making airboats the preferred method of transportation. With their flat bottoms and giant fan, they can scoot on both water and land.

Clive sat in the front seat while Jim drove on the elevated bench behind him. Daylight was fading fast, but Jim knew the waters around here better than his own kitchen. With all the water, there were really only a few places the monster could hide out. There was a mangrove island about a mile up where he knew wild hogs lived.

Local farms lost a few pigs years back, and over time they bred in the wild and became feral, monstrous beasts. They were the biggest headache for folks like Jim's family. The pigs were smarter than any dog he'd ever owned, and strong as an ox. Worst of all, they had no fear of people. They ate everything in their path, whether that be trash, deer, wild berries, or even livestock.

Jim brought the airboat up to the shoreline, eyeballing a dip in the grass along the embankment. He cut the engine and tapped Clive on the shoulder.

"Mind that gator hole," Jim said to Clive. "It's just on the other side of that embankment. You can see where they like to spring up on ya. This late at night, they'd surely be on the hunt for some of them wild pigs and deer. Grab me my gun and the hog light."

Clive didn't reply. He knew once his pa got in the mood for hunting there wasn't anything he could say that wouldn't sound foolish. He grabbed the flashlight and snapped on the green filter. It was the one thing he did know, that hogs couldn't see green lights very well, and the shadows it cast outlined their bodies better than red.

Clive handed his pa his hunting rifle from the gun crate under the bench and slung his own rifle over his shoulder. He grabbed the headlamp, snapped on the same filter, and passed it over to his pa. They were ready as they were gonna be.

It didn't take them long to find the trail of breadcrumbs left by the monster. An alligator carcass lay out on the wet ground not far from the water's edge. It was a big one, almost seventeen-feet long by Jim's guess. The body was still fresh, seeing as how few scavengers had arrived to pick through the meat. Jim knelt beside the reptile and rolled it over onto its back. Under its jaw, along the side of its neck, were three holes. Its body was badly scratched, and its front two legs were broken. Whatever did this was mean, strong, and brave as hell. Jim looked at his son, who shivered at the sight of such a massive gator, dead and drained of its blood no different than the chickens.

"This's almost scary as that time Curious ol' Bob snapped that bear's neck a few months back," Clive said, trying to shake off the willies. "You sure this ain't him?"

"Sure it ain't," Jim replied, spitting beside the carcass. "Curious ol' Bob has a thing for breakin' necks, not legs. Not on purpose, at least. And he don't bite none like this. His teeth are strong, but they flat like yours and mine. This thing has sharp teeth, needle teeth."

"What in the hell could have taken on such a big ol' alligator like this?"

"If I knew, surely I wouldn't be huntin' after it."

Jim got up and continued through the brush. He was agile for his size and age. His movements were practiced through years of swamp hunts and trapping out in the Everglades. Clive, however, was a lazy twig of a boy. Jim scarcely knew how a kid so dumb and pointless could have possibly come from his loins. Clive tripped over every branch, crunched every stick and leaf that crossed his path, and was the noisiest son-of-a-gun Jim ever heard.

"Boy!" he whispered intensely. "You don't shut the fuck up, I'll stick my boot so far up yer ass I'll kick your teeth out from behind."

Clive froze in place. His heart was already beating out of his chest, and his father always made good with his threats. Memories of the hot frying pan smacked against his ass still smoldered in the back of his mind, along with the lingering smell of burning hair. Clive could feel his hands grow clammy. As his pa turned and continued deeper into the brush, Clive fumbled his flashlight.

He dove for it, and by the time he stood up, his pa was gone. He looked ahead, then behind. The Everglades was a chorus of midnight insects and grumbling gators. He wanted to call out for his pa, but the taste of shoe leather tickled the back of his throat at the idea. Clive looked around. The trail behind him was swallowed by the dense woods, and the trail ahead was no better.

Panic was fast on his heels as Clive stormed through the brush. His feet splashed in the dense bog, his heartbeat and breath thundering in his ears. He was lost. Every overturned log, every fallen tree looked identical to the last. The green light cast strange and macabre shadows in the woods ahead. Spanish moss grew long tendrils and sharp teeth, while spaces between branches loomed over him like terrible eyes and yawning mouths.

Something splashed in the water behind him. He turned quickly, dropping his flashlight for his rifle. The light plunked in the water, casting him in darkness as he aimed his gun wildly. He breathed heavily through his nose, dripping with snot and chunky mucus. The water around him glowed green from the flashlight.

Great anacondas swam the waters around him while cottonmouth vipers hissed in his ear, fangs dripping with venom. Wild boars grunted and rutted in the shadows, their eyes glinting like false starlight. The water vibrated with the growls of hungry alligators. Clive spun in circles, pointing his gun at every strange sound around him. Sweat stung his eyes and his hands began to shake, but he held the rifle's wooden butt hard against his shoulder until he felt it might bruise him.

Something whimpered like a beaten dog in the distance. Clive lowered the rifle from his shoulder some and turned his ear toward the sound. He heard it again, a faint cry followed by the sound of grunting hogs. Whatever it was, it needed help. Clive dipped his hand in the water and grabbed the flashlight before running toward the sound.

It wasn't far, only a few yards deeper into the swamp. The sound of hogs grew louder, overpowering the whimpering animal. Clive came to a clearing. An animal the size of a Great Dane struggled with its back leg stuck in a bear trap while a pack of hogs encircled it. The beasts were massive swine and easily six feet long and over two hundred pounds each, with thick tusks the size of Clive's hand and coarse black and brown hair.

Clive counted five hogs against the trapped animal. He clicked off his flashlight and stuck it in his pocket. Raising his rifle, he held his breath, aimed at the largest boar in the pack, and squeezed the trigger. The gun clicked but did not fire. Quickly, Clive inspected his weapon. The safety was off, but as he looked inside the chamber a sickly feeling squirmed in his gut. He'd left the ammo back in the boat. His body was a wash of cold sweat as he fumbled around, thinking of what to do.

Then he remembered the camp knife and zip ties. He pulled them from his pocket and fastened the knife to the end of his rifle like a makeshift bayonet. Wielding the rifle like a spear, he charged the boars, screaming and cussing at the top of his lungs. Startled, the three smallest of the hogs turned and ran, but the big daddy pig stood its ground, turning to face him. Its eyes were wild in the moonlight as it bared its terrible, gnarled tusks and jagged teeth.

Clive attacked, thrusting the blade at the hog. The hog hopped to one side and rushed him. Clive fell, tripping in the muck as his feet treaded in the shallow water. The pig was on him in no time, as was the second largest. The big daddy bit into his calf, its teeth digging into his flesh and scratching bone. Clive hollered in pain, thrusting the knife's blade into the pig's side. The animal yelped, more in surprise than harm, as the hide was too thick for the blade to cut deep. The other pig made its attack, biting him on the shoulder.

This was the end, Clive knew it. His life flashed before his eyes in a series of clips and memories. He remembered his first blowjob when his sister was fourteen and his first real nut when his mother showed him the proper ways to love a woman.

Then came the nightmares as Pa beat his ass again and again. Sometimes it was for his own good, like when Pa caught him masturbating in the grits for the lunch special, while other beatings were simply 'cause Pa was drunk and his limp dick couldn't properly satisfy his mother. It was a short life, but one filled with wonderful and terrible memories.

The pig released its grip on his shoulder. Clive turned to see the pig being lifted into the air and tossed across the clearing. It was the animal stuck in the trap. It must have freed itself during the confusion. In the darkness, the thing looked like a mangy dog with brilliant blue and red eyes and a thin strip of wiry gray hair starting at its head and running down its back to its thin tail. Its pale blue skin was the texture of a shaved ball sack. It curled its thin lips to reveal three long, thin fangs and held up its strange raccoon-like hands armed with sharp claws.

The bizarre animal shrilled like a wet cat and walked like a squirrel, limping from the wound the trap made around its leg. The big daddy pig tackled it from the side. Clive got to his feet, his leg and shoulder burning where the boars got him. He picked up his rifle and ran up behind the hog as it snapped its jaws, barely held back by the animal's impressive strength.

With all his might, Clive brought the rifle down hard on the back of the boar's head. This time, the blade sank in deep. Its sharp edge found a space between vertebrae along the pig's spine and cut clean through it. The hog squealed and bucked wildly, but the wound was fatal, and life quickly drained from the feral beast. In seconds, the hog slumped over, dead, Clive's weapon still embedded in its back.

Clive fell to the ground beside it, exhausted. He closed his eyes, breathed in deeply, and lay against the carcass. Its wiry fur itched his ear and neck. Then he heard the other animal panting, the one stuck in the trap. He opened his eyes to see it staring down at him with massive dinner plate-sized eyes. Its red and blue irises shimmered in the moonlight.

The animal looked him over, questioningly, and licked Clive's face with its foot-long forked tongue. It was thin and slimy, like a wet snail dragging along his cheek and neck. The thin beads of saliva left his skin feeling numb and tingly.

"Ain't you the sweetest thing." Clive laughed at the tickling sensation. "Reckon you must be the thing that ate all our chickens. You don't look so bad."

Clive scratched the animal behind its fox-like ears. It shivered like a dog and kicked its good leg rapidly.

"I guess you need a name, don't ya?" Clive asked it. "How does Cooter work?"

5

THE HANGOVER WAS EPIC ENOUGH, but the shame seeped into Freddy's clothes like the stink of the strange man's cologne. Worst of all, it reminded him that last night was not a dream.

Freddy woke up in the bathtub, his naked chest covered in dried vomit, his pants soaked with piss. Every movement was agony, even blinking. He grunted, hoping the lazy vowels his throat coughed up were enough to alert someone he was still alive.

Jennifer stepped into the bathroom, looking him over with her hands on her hips. She was wearing her Wonder Woman shirt and short shorts. She said nothing, turned on the shower, and blasted her brother with cold water. Freddy jumped, shouting as the icy downpour cramped his legs, arms, and abdomen.

"We're leaving in five minutes, dipshit," she said coldly.

As she left, Freddy reached forward and turned on the hot water. He was shivering by the time the temperature warmed up. After his shower, he brushed his teeth, but there wasn't enough mouthwash in the world that could remove the taste of acrid puke and harsh liquor coating the roof of his mouth and tongue.

Freddy's eyes stung, not just from the hangover and bright sunlit room, but because he'd been sleeping with his contact lenses in all night. He kept a few extra pairs in his luggage, but that was on the other side of the hotel room, which felt miles away. He mustered all his strength and walked gingerly into the bedroom. His legs wobbled like Bambi on ice. Jennifer and Dean sat on the bed waiting for him. Winston wasn't with them.

"I fucked up." His throat stung as he spoke.

"Little bit," Dean said, demonstrating with his thumb and index finger.

"Did Winston leave?" Freddy asked.

"No," Jen said, refusing to look at him. "He went out for breakfast. We just wanted to make sure you didn't die in your sleep. Well, Dean did anyway."

"We're going to play it by ear," Dean said, giving Jen a sideglance before looking at Freddy. "Your relationship is none of our business until ya go and do something stupid like get drunk and have random sex with a stranger in a back alley. On *our* vacation."

"I don't think we had sex." Freddy took a seat on the guest bed across from them, still wrapped in his towel.

"Bro, you still cheated." Dean shrugged. "Winston isn't happy, and as you can see, neither is your sister. You gotta fix this, dude. We just started our road trip two days ago, and still have another two thousand eight hundred miles to get back to Anaheim. Your job is to fix this. I already pre-paid for the rental car and the hotels we'll be staying at.

"Dude, I've been planning this trip for over three years now, since your sister and I started dating. You were invited, despite my better judgment. I can't spring for Winston or you a ticket back to Cali without hurting the rest of the trip. From what I understand of your work situation, or lack thereof, I don't think you can either. So, we're going to have to make the best of it."

"Got it," Freddy replied.

"I'd have left you there," Jen said sharply. "Left you in that back alley to choke to death on your own vomit."

"I understand," Freddy replied.

Jen and Dean got up and went outside.

"We're grabbing breakfast and hitting the road," Dean said before stepping outside. "We packed everything else and left you some clothes on the office desk. Get dressed and let's get this thing going."

Winston wasn't at breakfast. Freddy was okay with that. He still needed time to process what to say, to figure out how he could possibly fix everything.

Even though the Cadillac Escalade Dean rented was a beast of a car, Freddy and Winston were pressed uncomfortably, almost on top of one another, just because of the luggage alone. Freddy regretted agreeing to come along. He'd only agreed because he wanted to see his sister's idea of "roughing it."

Dean pitched it as a road/camping trip across the whole country. Normally, camping was an activity his sister wouldn't have been caught dead doing. She hated parks and going outdoors so much she'd even said she'd rather be cremated and flushed down the toilet than buried in the filthy dirt.

Most of Jennifer's bags were just for camping stuff. Why wouldn't they be? To make the best of things, it became another excuse for her to go shopping. She'd bought designer hiking boots, UV protective shirts that acted like sunscreen, and other brand name active wear. They'd also brought some simple camping stuff, two tents, air mattresses, sleeping bags, a cook set with burners and a coffee percolator, some popcorn, and other rations.

Dean drove with Jennifer in the front. Freddy sat behind Dean with Winston in the middle seat, as the one behind Jennifer was folded down to accommodate even more suitcases. Those would be the souvenir bags where they could collect all the useless crap they couldn't live without.

Winston leaned against the bags with his headphones on, drifting in and out of sleep while Freddy looked out the darkly tinted windows. He'd been awake for a few hours, and his head was still pounding. Even inside the SUV, Freddy still needed sunglasses to protect his eyes from the daylight. He nursed a bottle of water and watched as the landscape raced by. After they crossed the Seven Mile Bridge from Key West to mainland Florida, they took US-1 to the turnpike to Miami.

Though Freddy and Jennifer both grew up with Mexican parents, Jennifer was the only one of them who knew Spanish. He'd given up trying to learn when he was five. He understood it well enough but couldn't speak enough to ask anything other than where the bathroom was. Jennifer wanted to sample the beach life, culture, history, and cuisine. What they found was a tangled knot of overpasses, construction, and congestion.

By eleven, it was already getting late, and Miami was a bust. Dean turned off the interstate and made his way toward Alligator Alley.

"We're leaving?" Jennifer asked.

"There's no way we're going to do any of the things you wanted with all this traffic," Dean tried to explain.

"This is bullshit," she complained.

"I know you're upset about everything," Dean tried to calm her down. "But, baby, we still got a long way to go and a lot more stuff to see."

"Why don't we just pull off anywhere and find some hole-in-the-wall Cuban place for lunch?" Freddy suggested.

"Bro," Dean was losing his cool, "that's not in the plan! I figured we'd already be at the beach for at least an hour by now, soaking up some sun, and we'd be on our way towards the west coast. I already had shit lined up for . . . for an airboat tour."

"The hell is an airboat?" Jennifer sneered. "You know I don't like boats."

"It's not a cruise or anything like that. It's like a canoe, only it's got a big fan on it."

"You're not selling it any better, Papi."

"I made reservations for a private tour in the Everglades around two. It's already, like, two hours to get there from here and we just don't have time. "

"You really suck at this whole vacation thing," Freddy said to Dean.

"Shut up!" Dean shouted. "Dude, I don't wanna hear a goddamn thing from you. We're going on an airboat tour. If we have time to eat, we'll eat."

"You're just gonna let him talk to me like that?" Freddy asked his sister.

She didn't reply, only sat in the front passenger seat with her arms folded across her chest.

"Snacks are in one of the coolers," Dean offered. "Maybe you can just munch on those until we get to where we're going?"

"Yeah," Freddy said, looking at the mound of crap around him. "If I can find the damn thing."

After some digging, Freddy found the cooler under the mountain of luggage.

"There's a Pride Fest going on tonight in Las Olas?" Winston scrolled through his smartphone.

"That should be fun!" Jennifer exclaimed.

"Didn't we get enough of that in Key West?" Dean posited.

"Enough of what?" Winston asked.

"Enough of the drinking and partying in the streets," Dean quickly defended. "God, I can't believe I just said that."

"Say that again," Jennifer scoffed. "Out loud, slowly. Of course we didn't get enough drinking and partying with my gay boos!"

"I had a whole thing planned," Dean tried. "I'd have to call and reschedule everything."

"It's okay, Papi," Jennifer whispered into his ear, rubbing his thigh. "We'll have some fun."

She could feel the goosebumps prickling the back of his neck as she kissed him there. Freddy rolled his eyes, annoyed and grossed out by his sister's public display of affection. He honestly couldn't think of how this trip could possibly get any worse.

6

IT WAS A HARDER TRIP back home than Clive expected. The Everglades was shallow enough that one could walk most of it, but Cooter found himself, or herself, swimming through most of it. Cooter happened to be pretty good at it, considering how badly the creature was hurt. That was when Clive realized he had no idea if Cooter was a boy or a girl. He gave one quick inspection of the plumbing and quickly decided it was a girl.

It was almost dawn by the time they made it home. The airboat was still missing, so Pa must have still been out there. He knew Pa wouldn't spend too much time looking for him. He'd just as well leave him out there to die. Wouldn't have been the first time he'd done it, or the last.

"Now what am I gonna do with you?" Clive asked Cooter. "I can't have you hangin' around here when Pa gets home. He don't like dogs much. I got a feelin' he'd be cross if I brought back the cocksucker that done sucked down all our chickens. I forgive you. You done saved my life. I owe you that.

"I got it! I'll keep you in the shed! Not long, I promise. Just till Pa cools his heels some. He's got a devil of a temper."

Clive led Cooter into the shed. It was a rickety old thing about as old as the house. Inside was grim and dark, but Cooter's eyes glowed so bright, he could make out rough shadows and silhouettes of the tools and supplies Pa kept inside. He cleared a space under a bench just long enough for her to fit, laid down some tarp for bedding, and showed Cooter her bed for the night. Cooter sniffed it, looked at Clive, and lay down.

Truck lights spilled through the cracks in the shed.

Pa was home.

"Okay," Clive said. "I gotta go. I'll be back in the mornin' when I wake up. Don't make a sound. You got that?" Cooter tilted her head. Clive petted her sweaty, leathery skin and kissed her on the cheek. "I'll be back."

Clive stepped out of the shed as Jim worked at unhitching the airboat trailer.

"Where the hell you been?" Jim demanded. "I looked for you almost twenty goddamn minutes."

"I got lost," Clive said, placing his hands in his overall pockets.

"No shit," Jim replied. "And your dumb ass forgot to give me my fuckin' bullets. What the hell kinda hunter remembers his rifle, but forgets his goddamn ammunition?"

"I'm sorry, Pa." Clive looked at his feet, kicking the dirt.

"Your ass is lucky I keep some shells in my back pocket," Jim said as he hopped in the back of his truck. "'Cause this here hog nearly got the drop on your ol' man. I hate to say it, but I think this is the fucker that killed them hens. Got three teeth in its whole head."

"I saw that pig before," Clive thought up his lie quick. "It jumped me. Got me good, too. I'm glad you killed it."

"How bad it get ya?" Jim asked, looking at Clive's wounds.

"Got my leg and my shoulder." Clive showed him his bites.

"Not bad," Jim let a faint smile creep across his tobacco-stained lips as he popped in his corn pipe. "Scars are the first thing ya need to be a real man. Those'll heal up pretty good, and you might actually have somethin' to show for it. Shame you didn't remember them bullets. You might have caught this hog yerself. Ha! Who the fuck am I kiddin'? Go get cleaned up and we can field dress this pig tomorrow. I just gotta drop this carcass in the cooler."

"I can do it!"

"I gotta bleed the fucker first."

"I can do that too!"

"Since when?"

"Whatcha mean?"

"Since when did you ever wanna set up my kill for dressin'?"

"I know how bad I screwed up, Pa. I just wanna make it up."

"You can start by stayin' outta my goddamn way."

"Please? I wanna help. I'll do whatever ya ask me."

"Whatever I ask of you?"

Clive gulped and said, "Yep."

"Good. You can start by drainin' this here hog in the shed. Don't want no animals gettin' its carcass. After that you gotta wash it down and drop it in the cooler quick. Gonna smell like shit come mornin', otherwise. Then wash the truck and clean off the boat. Ask and you shall receive!"

Jim patted Clive hard on his bloody shoulder. The shock of pain knocked the air out of him.

$$\longleftrightarrow$$

The pig already smelled like shit. Blood had collected in the bed of the truck and would have to be dealt with before the sun came up. Clive grabbed the hog by the legs. It was heavier than he'd expected and his shoulder burned as he struggled with the carcass.

Even with all his strength, he was barely able to drag the hundred-pound animal out of the truck. It slipped from his hands and landed hard on the ground.

Clive cursed and grabbed it again, huffing and grunting as he pulled it up to the shed. Cooter scuttled around inside, sniffing the air. Clive opened the shed and braced himself as Cooter tried to jump for the pig.

"Watch it!" Clive said in a loud whisper. "I gotta get him inside, first!"

Cooter licked her lips with her long tongue at the sight of it. Clive dragged the body the rest of the way. It was then that he saw the magnitude of the problem. He'd have to pick up the hundred-pound hog and hang it on the meat hook by himself.

Clive spat on his hands—making sure to get enough wind in his lungs—and rubbed his palms together before grabbing the porker's legs. He huffed and gritted his teeth, working every ounce of strength till he felt his back almost give way, but the pig would not budge. It was useless. He was a failure all right. Just like Pa said.

Cooter licked Clive's face. Her tongue was rough like slimy sandpaper. With her raccoon-like hands, Cooter grabbed the hog's legs, and with some effort, lifted the beast into the air. Clive's face lit up like a Christmas tree as he helped Cooter get the animal on the meat hook.

Clive grabbed the knife from the table, and with his back turned only a second, Cooter bit down on the hog's neck. By the time Clive saw, the pig was almost totally drained of blood.

"Hey!" Clive said, pushing Cooter out of the way. "Knock it off! I gotta do this right or Pa's gonna tan my hide."

Clive placed a pan under the pig and slit the animal's throat, trying to hide Cooter's bite marks as best he could with his cut.

What little blood was left came out in a slow trickle, barely filling the bottom of the pan. Cooter was quick to lap up the drippings.

"I guess you'll be all right by yourself," Clive said, watching Cooter polish off the last of the blood before turning his attention back to the carcass. "Ya know, if Pa has to come in here to break down the pig, I don't know how he's gonna handle bumping into you. Shit."

Clive's smile soured at the realization of the work ahead of him. He would have to finish butchering the pig so Pa wouldn't have to use the shed. Clive rolled up his sleeve and got to work.

Cooter wasn't your typical dog. She had no interest in the meat whatsoever, which made Clive's job of skinning and hacking up the carcass that much easier. He de-gloved the skin from the body and quartered the meat before placing the trimmings in the icebox in the back of the shed. After the hour or so it took him, he was hot, sweaty, and exhausted.

"Okay, I'm gonna check up on you when I get up. You be good in here and try not to make any noises."

Clive grabbed the tools he'd need for the morning—some new chicken wire, nails, hammer, and a few planks of wood. Cooter had already lain back down on the tarp and was fast asleep, her wrinkled skin sagging like an old man's jowls. Clive scratched his new friend's belly, watching in delight as she kicked her back legs, and giggled at how silly she looked.

Clive always wanted a dog and Pa was always against it. "Just another expense," he'd say, or something else for him to take care of 'cause Clive was so damn useless. This was different. Cooter was more than just a good dog; she was Clive's best friend. After all, isn't that what all good dogs are?

7

"**YOU BOOKED US ON SEPARATE** floors?" Jennifer yelled at Dean.

"It was last minute!" Dean replied, trying his hardest not to lose it in the middle of the valet drop-off. "Dude, you guys wanted to pick a hotel in the area, this one had reservations, but I couldn't get them on the same floor. It's no big deal. Your brother's a big boy."

"How many rooms did you get?" she asked.

"I got two."

"Did you even think to ask if they wanted the same fucking room? *Puto loco*, what were you thinking? So insensitive!"

"Do you have any idea how much these rooms cost?"

"Doesn't matter."

Freddy and Winston stood by the car next to the valet driver. They stared at Jen and Dean while they shouted back and forth.

"Whose side are you on?" asked the valet.

"Neither," Freddy crossed his arms. "We both lose this one. We have to drive back with them."

"That sucks." The valet pinched his lips like a duck and nodded.

"Let's just get our shit into the room and go from there!" Dean finally lost it.

"But ya know the make-up sex is gonna be bomb," the valet nodded again.

"Fuck you," Freddy punched him in the arm. "That's my sister."

"Kidding!" He laughed. "Still . . . sucks to be you."

"You guys ready to kiss and make up yet?" Winston asked as Dean stomped over to the car for their luggage.

"I'll get a cart!" The valet rushed away.

"Here's your room key," Dean pushed the plastic card onto Freddy's chest. "You're on the second floor."

"What floor did you guys get?" Winston asked.

"Twelfth," Dean huffed before Jennifer came over.

"All right, let's go. What are we waiting for?" she said in one long breath.

"Here you go," the valet said with a bellman and two carts beside him. "We'll get this loaded up and get you guys to your rooms."

Jennifer and Winston went ahead to the rooms while Freddy and Dean helped load the carts.

"She's pretty pissed," Freddy said to Dean.

"Yep," Dean quickly replied. "Why do you think she's so pissed?"

"Do I wanna know?" Freddy asked.

"Bro, you did just cheat on your boyfriend," Dean huffed as he grabbed a heavy piece of Jennifer's luggage. "In front of God and everyone. It's not me she's really pissed at, ya know?"

"I kinda figured."

"Dude, just leave it to me, all right? I'll try to talk to her tonight after she's cooled down over a few drinks. Let her decompress a little after that long ass trip in the car, and we'll play it by ear."

Dean patted Freddy's shoulder.

"I got your back," he smiled. "Don't worry."

The room Freddy and Winston shared was small but at least had two beds. It was a simple room, with a bathroom, TV, cheap dresser and nightstand, and an AC turned all the way down. Freddy took a deep breath, held it, and released it in a heavy sigh as he pulled in their luggage. Winston lay on the bed, flipping through the TV. Freddy's heart pounded in his chest. His hands were sweaty. There were so many things buzzing around in his head he couldn't think of what he could possibly say.

"They said they'd meet us downstairs in about an hour." Freddy felt like such a tool.

"All right," Winston said.

Freddy stood in the doorway, looking the man over. He loved Winston's arms and calves. Florida was always shorts and t-shirt weather, and he could see every curve and crease in Winston's defined calves and triceps. Freddy bit his lip, watching Winston chew his inner cheek. It was a nervous tic, a tell he'd learned early on when he'd brought up meeting each other's family.

"You just gonna stand there?" Winston asked. "It's awkward enough as it is."

"Sorry," Freddy said.

"Will you stop fucking saying that?!" he snapped.

"I-I mean, I don't know what else *to* say?"

"Find another word. It's getting old. I get it, you're sorry. That doesn't take back shit."

"I can't take it back. I know I can't. But I just, I don't know what to do."

"Don't do anything. And especially don't say you're sorry."

"All right."

Freddy rolled the suitcase over and sat on his bed.

"Do you wanna talk about it?" Freddy asked.

"Nope," Winston said flatly, his eyes never once looking away from the TV.

"Then what do you wanna talk about?"

"The weather? I don't care. I'm not in the mood."

Freddy caught himself before saying sorry again, but only just barely. The comment, or the attempt, didn't go unnoticed. Winston looked in his direction, expecting the words to fumble out any second, but Freddy held it together, his lips curled as they went to speak the new swear word of the day. Winston threw the remote onto Freddy's bed before getting up and slipping his shoes back on.

"Where you going?" Freddy asked.

"Out," was his only reply.

Winston grabbed his copy of the room key from the dresser and left. The TV was still on, some history documentary on the Battle of the Bulge. Almost two hundred thousand people lost their lives in only forty-one days. In forty-one seconds, Freddy knew exactly how they all felt.

◄——————————————►

Dean spared no expense on the room he'd booked for himself and Jennifer. It was the top-floor executive suite overlooking the Tarpon River. It was a grand space with a living room, bedroom, and a large master bath with jetted soaker tub and a shower tiled in fine marble.

Though she wouldn't say it out loud, Jennifer was impressed. She'd already undressed and prepared herself for a hot shower by the time Dean made it up with her bags. She closed the bathroom door and locked it. She needed her space to decompress. Jennifer put her hair in a bun and stepped into the steaming water.

Showers were her sanctuary. When the door was closed and the water was running, no one disturbed her in fear of a painful death. Dean always made fun of her little ritual, calling her a perv. Truth is, she wasn't, and her showers weren't some kind of masturbation session. She needed the time to collect herself and clear her headspace. This weekend was proving to be one hell of a rollercoaster, and it'd only just started.

Lathering herself with body wash, she couldn't help but think about Freddy, hoping he was okay and that his heart wasn't too broken about Winston turning him down. She understood why. The two only dated a few months, and Freddy came out of the closet as he fell in love with Winston. It was too soon, too much, too everything.

As much as Jennifer wanted to be mad about the cheating, he was still her brother, and it was her job to kick his ass when he got out of line. As she rinsed off, all her anger and frustration melted away like the thick lather tingling against her skin. She sighed and stepped out of the shower, drying herself off with the luxurious bath towel.

Jennifer decided she'd been too hard on the kid. She'd given him his tough love, now it was time to reel him in and comfort him and explain how bad he'd gone and fucked things up.

Dean sat on the bed outside the bathroom. She'd almost completely forgotten about him and seeing him reminded her how angry she still was with him.

"How are you feeling?" he asked.

She said nothing and went to her luggage on the table by the bed. As mad as she was at him, the sight of his strong arms and colorful tribal tattoos had an effect on her unlike any man she'd been with. Jennifer knew exactly how strong he was, and that knowledge both scared her and turned her on. If only she could convince him to be a little . . . kinkier.

Jennifer slipped on her matching pink thong panties and bra. Ignoring Dean as he looked up at her with puppy eyes. Pride is thicker than blood.

"Everything okay?" Dean asked.

"Do you think it's okay?" Jennifer didn't even courtesy a glance.

"Hun, if I knew I wouldn't have asked." Dean shook his head.

"If you have to ask, then you'll never know."

"Why are we fighting?"

"Because you are insensitive."

"Hun, I told you already. This place was booked solid. And these rooms are not cheap."

"Don't 'hun' me. You could have at least told me before you booked the room."

"We're both really tired from all this driving. I needed a break, you needed a break, everyone had to get out of that damn car."

"I guess."

"What's really bothering you?"

"You know exactly what's bothering me."

"I get it, he's your brother, and he fucked up. We're on vacation. He's a grown ass man, though. He needs to learn to deal with his problems."

"He's my little brother, *cabrón*. Watch what comes out your mouth."

"You're not the only one disappointed in him."

"Fine! Fine. Look, since our parents died, it's only been him and me. I have to look out for him. He's a fuck-up, but he's my *familia*, we have to protect our own. Maybe we shouldn't do this differently. Maybe we should just take him home and start this trip over."

"What are you talking about? We've been planning this for over a year now!"

"But he comes first, you understand?"

"Normally, yes, but he's gotta figure some shit out first."

"What do you mean?"

"I had a talk with him while we packed luggage. He seems super upset and sorry, but I'm not so sure. Like . . . he keeps saying sorry, but I don't feel like he really is."

"I'm gonna kick his fucking ass."

"No! Don't do that!"

"Why? He thinks he can do whatever he wants when he doesn't get his way? I'll show him exactly what he gets."

"He needs to learn on his own."

"But what about Winston? You think this is good for him to have to deal with my brother's bullshit?"

"If Winston wants to leave, he can leave, but we can't afford to just ship him back. This detour really hurt my spending money. We were already on a thin budget as it was. We were gonna do some touristy stuff today and drive over to Orlando for the theme parks tomorrow. I can't cancel those, I'll lose the deposit."

"So what? We make him suffer just because of money?"

"I'm not saying that! I'm saying we have already sacrificed enough of our trip because your brother can't figure out what he wants. This is his chance to show his true colors. I know he loves Winston. I know he does. He's got that look in his eyes, the same one I had when I first met you. I know how your bro feels, and maybe he's just confused about it. If we step in, he could lose his chance of showing that to Winston."

"You think so?"

"I do."

"But what about the other guy? You said he was obsessed?"

"Maybe. Maybe he was just confused. He'd been drinking."

"And you think drinking tonight is gonna help?"

"Yeah, but Winston wasn't drinking much either. I think they both need to get loose and just see what happens."

Jennifer wanted to believe the best in her brother. All Dean needed to do was suggest it, and she'd take it wherever he led her. He knew all too well the power her brother had on her and knew exactly how to position his argument. After all, Dean wasn't about to let this whole trip get any more fucked up just because of some horny kid who couldn't keep his dick in his pants, unless that kid was himself.

8

CLIVE WAS EXHAUSTED, BUT THE excitement of his new best friend kept him up most of the night. After only passing out for a few hours, he woke up and was back outside. He didn't want Pa to have any reason to go in the shed, so after breakfast he went right to work on the henhouse.

Pa was soon up and loading the truck with supplies.

"Goin' huntin' for more cocksuckers?" Clive asked.

"Nah," Pa guffed. "Laid out traps last night. Course, you'd know that if you hadn't run off and got lost. Better that way, I suppose. I might have killed you on the spot when I found my rifle had no ammo. I dunno why your ass is fixin' the henhouse when it ain't got no fucking hens in it."

"I figured—"

"Well, you can stop that. You tryin' to think is about as useful as a screen door on a submarine. I ain't lookin' for no more cocksuckers today. I'm goin' over to grab Ol' Billy Boy. We goin' snake huntin'. With them chickens gone, we need to get us some new ones. Ain't got no tourists in the restaurant, so we ain't got no money."

"But I ain't ever hunted snakes before."

"Can't be any worse at it than ya are hog huntin'. I swear I'll make a man outta you yet, boy. Ya can't shoot, but at least I know you can run. You gotta be fast to catch these devils."

"I'm not sure I'll be any good, Pa."

"Course you ain't gonna be any fuckin' good! I don't even know how my seed could build such a worthless man. Probably got that from your mother's side. I aim to correct that. Now, quit pussy-footin' around with that empty chicken coop and help me with this truck."

They loaded the truck with empty buckets with screw-on lids, over a dozen pillowcases, and three empty plastic truck toolboxes. Filled up, the two hopped in the cab and set off down the road. Billy Boy didn't live too far. It was only a twenty-minute drive, which was still closer than the nearest grocery store.

Billy Boy lived in a single-wide trailer with his wife, Clara. Clive only saw the woman once or twice, but never outside of the home because she wouldn't fit out her own front door. The woman was wide at the hips, tits, and shoulders. Billy Boy couldn't have been any more different. Then again, crystal meth would do that to a man. His breath stank like melted plastic, his hair and body were thin and wiry, and his skin was crackled and covered in sores.

His trailer was a piece of shit. The siding was black and green with mold. Clive could hear the floors creak as the people moved around inside. Although none of the windows opened, you could feel a cold breeze whistle out of the cracks from the window-shaker AC units rattling around. Spit, duct tape, and bad habits seemed to be the only thing keeping the home in place. During hurricanes, it was probably the missus inside that kept the thing from going up like a box kite.

"This that mistake you keep talkin' 'bout?" Billy Boy said as he stepped out of the mobile home. "Yep, he looks about as dumb as you was talkin'."

"That's my boy." Pa shook his head in disappointment, holding onto his pipe.

Billy Boy sucked the three blue teeth protruding from his gums like cypress knees. He looked Clive over, unimpressed as he spat a wad of chaw beside him. Clive wasn't any more impressed with Billy Boy. The man stank of burnt plastic and old spat-up chewing tobacco. White hairs peppered his leathery skin from his nose all the way to the knuckles of his toes.

"You know what a snake looks like, boy?" Billy Boy asked.

"Don't confuse the runt," Pa laughed as he readied his little .22 rifle.

"I think so," Clive answered, his face and hands sweaty as he looked into Billy Boy's bloodshot eyes. "They like lizards with no legs. I've seen 'em before."

"I ain't talkin no cottonmouths swimmin' in your outhouse." Billy Bob pressed two fingers to Clive's chest. "I'm talkin' mean motherfuckers. Snakes as big as twenty feet. Snakes that can swallow alligators. Look at you in them boots. Ain't you just cute. Boy, when I was your age, I was huntin' gators barehanded!"

Billy Boy held up his hand. His index and ring finger were gone past the first knuckle, and his pinky was missing after the second.

"Shut the fuck up!" Pa chuckled. "You know you only lost them fingerbangin' the missus!"

Billy Boy cackled like an old hag with phlegm in the back of his throat.

The front door of the mobile home swung open violently. Billy Boy jumped in surprise. Clara loomed in the threshold, her shoulders hunched up to her ears so she could peek through the doorframe.

"Billy!" she barked like a quarterback. "You scrawny piece of shit, better not keep me waitin'. I got dinner boilin', and if you ain't back by sundown, your ass ain't eatin'!"

"Yes ma'am," Billy Boy gulped.

Clive watched the fat on her arms flapping in the air as she reached for the door and slammed it closed. He could have sworn he saw the trailer rock back and settle into place as she moved toward the other side of the home.

Pa laughed hysterically and Billy Boy looked at the ground like a beaten dog.

"Let's get on with this." Billy Boy twitched as he walked up to them.

"And I thought my old lady spoiled like milk in the sun!" Pa laughed. "At least that means I get cottage cheese. You got the whole dead cow!"

"Shut it!" Billy Boy snapped.

"What's a'matter?" Pa continued. "Missus gotcha balls?"

"It ain't funny!"

"What happens when she finishes dinner and you ain't home? She gonna eat you too? Least then you'd get to be a pain in her ass one last time, on the way out!"

"I told ya, it ain't funny, Jim!"

Clive wanted no part of their insult fest. All he could think about was Cooter locked up in that shed all day.

"Fuck's the matter with you, boy?" Pa snapped at Clive. "The hell you so quiet for? Like you got more important things to do?"

"None really," Clive shook his head.

"Now you listen here," Pa pointed at Clive. "We're about to go out there and make us some good money. You best not fuck this up. You understand me, boy?"

"Yes, Pa." Clive nodded.

"Good thing we ain't gotta go far," Pa snuck a look back at Billy Boy, "'cause you'd never wanna keep the missus waitin', now would ya?"

"Fuck you, Jim." Billy Boy spat on the floor. "Fuck you."

"You got your shit with you, right?" Pa asked Billy Boy.

"Sure as shit," Billy Boy replied before walking to the side of the trailer to grab something. "Stole this from the Wel-Mart up the road. Use it there for them high hanging clothes. Figured it'd make a good snake stick."

Billy Boy showed them a long metal rod about four feet long with a bent hook at one end and a rubber grip at the other.

"That'll do for some ornery sucker," Pa smiled. "The boy ain't gonna use it. Still gotta prove his self. Clive! You gonna catch one of these serpents barehanded."

"How big are they?" Clive asked, tentatively.

"I told you, big enough to swallow a whole gator," Billy Boy chuckled. "You ready, boy?"

"No, he ain't," Pa remarked. "Boy's about as lazy as a dead horse."

Clive didn't say anything. Pa was always like that. Once he got rolling, there was no stopping the mean words slipping through those lips. Clive knew it was best to keep his head down and his own mouth shut.

Pa only stopped to pull out his phone to call up the Fish and Wildlife Service. He told them they were on the clock and turned on the GPS on his phone so they could track exactly where they were hunting. The hourly wage was minimal, but that didn't matter. The real money was in the snake catching. It was fifty dollars for every four-foot snake, and twenty-five dollars more for every foot over. You find a nest, it was an automatic two hundred for destroying it and taking back the eggs.

The men grabbed a few buckets and some pillowcases and entered the glades just behind Billy Boy's trailer.

9

WINSTON WAS ALREADY OUTSIDE WHEN the rest of the group came down. He didn't say anything outwardly, but Freddy knew him well enough to know he wanted to go home. He was done with this vacation. Freddy wanted to say something, but he'd thought about what Dean told him. Jennifer didn't deserve to have her vacation cut short. He made sure he did what he could to patch things up and just make it work.

Freddy dressed in a white undershirt with a brown jacket and brown dress boots. He fixed his hair in a rock-hard pompadour, the same look he'd worn when he'd met Winston for the first time. Jennifer dressed in a lime green party dress with blue high heels, gold and cobalt bracelets with matching earrings, and a small blue- and green-striped purse. Dean wore a white shirt with black jeans and a black blazer, his hair perfectly faded and gelled so the strongest winds couldn't move a single strand of hair.

Winston wore the same thing he had all day. It wasn't just hot; it was humid as well. He looked over everyone's outfits and pitied how sweaty and hot they'd be in only a few minutes.

"You guys ready?" Freddy asked.

Winston didn't reply.

"Where to first?" Dean asked.

"There's a big thing happening at the Euro Club," Winston commented, looking at his phone. "We can take an Uber that way and see what we find?"

"Sounds good," Jennifer smiled. "Let's go, people!"

Winston got on his phone and ordered the ride. In less than ten minutes, they'd arrived at downtown Himmarshee Street and Nugent Avenue. Rainbow streamers and flags were hung across the Original Fat Cats, multicolored lights and prismatic lasers flickered against most of the buildings and plaza walls, and rave music thundered through the streets. Up the street on the same block as the eBar Club 13, SWAY Nightclub, and Stache Drinking Den and Coffee Bar, was Revolution Live. A concert was going on, with music in heavy contrast to the club scene they'd stepped into.

Heavy metal blasted from the concert hall as some of the fans mingled with the clubbers, wearing all-black concert shirts, corpse paint, and leather. The roads were closed, so people drank and partied out in the middle of the street, wearing tie-dye, tightly fitted club wear, or almost nothing at all. It was like Key West all over again, and Freddy felt more uncomfortable than ever before.

The entrance to the Euro Club was tucked away down a narrow alley. If not for their phone's directions, they might have missed it altogether. Dean paid their cover fee, and the four stepped into a world of neon sex.

Multicolored LEDs illuminated the room in a kaleidoscope of evolving colors and patterns. The bar was clad with blown glass and mirrored liquor shelves. The counter was white marble, as were the floors and walls, glinting with bits of crystal and glitter. Even the tables were fitted with lighting that changed with no rhyme or reason, often in contrast to whatever hip-hop or techno the DJ mixed.

This was neither Freddy's nor Winston's scene. The people who attended danced in ways that made the two uncomfortable. They pounded hips, grunted, groaned, and shouted whoops of orgasmic triumph. It was every sexual act done without taking off any clothes.

Jennifer, however, was elated. Dancing was her passion, and the raunchier it was, the more she enjoyed it. She pulled Dean into the fray. He went willingly and protested little as Jennifer twerked her ass in his crotch while another woman groped her breasts and swiveled her hips to the bass beat pounding in everyone's chest.

The sight of his sister playacting sex made Freddy queasy.

"This isn't what I had in mind," Freddy shouted in Winston's ear.

"No," Winston agreed. "Not really."

"Let's go to the bar," Freddy suggested before speaking to himself. "Maybe get something to calm our nerves."

Winston nodded, and they walked around and through the crowds. At the bar, Freddy ordered a vodka cranberry, and Winston a Captain and Coke. Freddy downed his drink in one go and ordered another. Winston said nothing, only shaking his head. They sat on the stools and watched the crowd. Strobe lights came on, and the room made Winston feel lightheaded. He sipped his drink. It tasted funny, but it was liquor, so he drank it anyway.

"What are you thinking?" Freddy asked Winston the only question he could think of.

He finished his drink again and ordered another.

"About being anywhere but here," Winston replied, watching a lesbian couple wrapped around each other, kissing passionately.

"Yeah," Freddy said, sipping his drink.

"I don't know what to tell you," Winston tried to explain, watching the carbonation in his drink fizz.

"Tell me anything." Freddy took a heavy swig of his drink, finished it, and ordered another. He was beginning to feel lightheaded, but it didn't matter. "I know I fucked up. But I want to fix this."

"What's there to fix?"

"Do you still love me?"

"Why did you ask me that?"

"Because I need to know. Do you love me? I don't . . . care . . . if you don't want to marry me. You're absolutely right; it was way too fucking early. But I need to know, do you love me?"

"If you asked me a week ago, I'd have said yes, right on the spot, no question, no hesitation. After what you did with a total stranger?"

"I will do anything. Just ask me. I'd walk off a cliff, jump off a bridge. Hell, I'd run across this room butt-ass naked. Winston, tell me what to do."

"Give me space."

Freddy felt the bottom drop from under his heart. His hands and face went clammy and began to shake.

"You're breaking up with me?" he asked.

"I don't know." Winston shook his head. "I just can't be around you right now."

Winston sipped his drink, wincing at the bitter taste. Some of the ice melted and watered it down, much like the feelings he felt when he looked at Freddy for the first time all night. Freddy's eyes were wide and glossy. It was as if all the joy seeped out through his lips.

Something else was wrong. Winston felt dizzy and more

lightheaded than before. His body felt very heavy, and he was suddenly very tired. He was going to pass out. Standing to leave, his legs felt weak and he collapsed onto the floor. Freddy shot over, cradling his head in his arms. He looked up for the bartender, but he'd vanished. Freddy looked at Winston's glass, spilled on the floor. Sitting in the ice was a mostly dissolved white tablet.

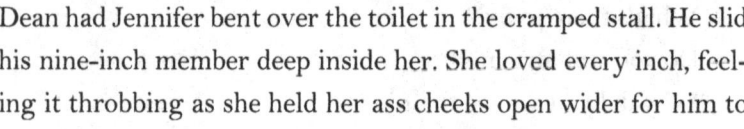

Dean had Jennifer bent over the toilet in the cramped stall. He slid his nine-inch member deep inside her. She loved every inch, feeling it throbbing as she held her ass cheeks open wider for him to fuck her deeper. She didn't care about the toilet or the crowd of people waiting to use it. All she cared about was Dean's fat cock slipping in and out with machine-like tempo.

Dean was an ass, she couldn't deny it, but he was her best fuck. She came not twice but three times in that stall before someone pounded on the door.

"Wait your fucking turn!" Dean shouted.

"Winston!" Freddy shouted. "Something happened!"

"Fuck me," Dean said, pulling out suddenly.

"What the hell?" Jennifer said, sliding her skirt back into place while Dean played with his hard cock, still slimy with all her juices.

"I think someone roofied his drink!" Freddy yelled through the door.

Jennifer didn't wait. She swung the door open while Dean fumbled with his dick, trying frantically to shoehorn it back in his tight pants.

"Where is he?" Jennifer demanded.

"I already called an ambulance," Freddy said, grabbing her by the arm and taking her to him.

"Really?" Dean said with his cock only half in his pants.

A line formed outside the bathroom. Woman stared gleefully at his throbbing meat as he hurried to tuck it down and into his pants. As he walked toward the bar, he was met with a chorus of whistles and catcalls. Jennifer ignored them, but Dean half-smiled and took them as compliments.

Fuck, he thought to himself. *Another night without a goddamn nut.*

10

"**I'LL GIVE YOU TO THE** count of three," Jim scolded Clive. "To stick your goddamn hands in that hole and yank out the fuckin' snake. One . . . two . . ."

Clive closed his eyes and pinched his lips before shoving his hand in the brush pile. There was a hole the size of a coffee mug where Billy Boy said he'd seen a snake slither into. Clive hated snakes, and Jim knew that. This was his son's last chance to prove himself a man. So far, he was royally fucking that up.

Clive twisted his arm inside the hole, his finger cupped together so nothing inside might bite them off. Jim watched his son sweating like a pig, moaning and crying that he couldn't feel anything.

"Deeper, boy!" Jim laughed. "If that were some pussy, you'd be in that shit up to your ankles!"

"Pa!" Clive begged, his voice full of panic. "Please, Pa! I wanna go home! I wanna stop!"

"I dunno where I went wrong." Jim shook his head, looking at Billy Boy for support.

Clive let out a high shrill scream. Billy Boy and Jim shook their heads in shame.

"Something touched me!" he yelled. "I felt it! It touched my finger!"

"Well grab it!" Jim demanded, holding his .22 at the ready.

Tears rained down Clive's cheeks as his fingers clasped around whatever it was he'd felt. With a heavy grunt, and all his strength, he yanked it from the brush pile. It was the heaviest animal he'd ever felt, and the skin was cold and smooth. It was a python all right, the brown and tan patterns on its scales slowly becoming visible as he dragged it from its hole, wailing like a child with every inch he pulled.

The snake whipped its body quickly as a head peered from out of the brush pile. Clive screamed a high-pitched squeal. If his fear of Pa wasn't greater than his fear of snakes, he'd have dropped the damn thing and run all the way home. But Pa towered over him with his gun in hand, and Clive held onto that devil like his life depended on it.

The snake sniffed the air with its fiendish forked tongue. Clive's body quivered. The snake looked directly at him and lunged. It was quick as lightning and, in a second, grabbed him by the arm in its powerful jaws. Clive could feel the rows of tiny dagger-like teeth dig into his skin. Its skull was easily the size of a German shepherd's head, and the damn thing was strong as hell. Clive fell over and the snake coiled around his body.

Jim and Billy Boy laughed at the sight as Clive flopped about like a fish out of water, screaming bloody murder. More of the snake's body wormed its way out of the brush pile. It was over fourteen feet of muscle, scales, and hate. Clive could feel the reptile's weight on his chest like a pile of bricks. It worked its long body around his legs and arms and flexed with all its strength. His toes tingled with pins and needles and his calves went numb.

Clive punched and scratched, but the reptile's armor was too tough. Then he went for the eyes, grabbing them hard with his thumbs.

"That's it!" Jim cheered. "Stop fightin' like a bitch! Fight like a man! Fight dirty, coward!"

All at once the snake released its bite and grip over his body. It pulled back, but now Clive had the upper hand and held on tight. He yanked it back by its head, the pain in his arm almost unbearable. There was no choice, he had to push through, to fight through the pain.

Clive held its face with one hand, his thumb still in the serpent's eye, and jumped on it from behind like he'd seen alligator wranglers do to their gators. He pressed its head into the dirt while Jim moseyed on over. He placed his .22 to the snake's forehead and pulled the trigger. Clive felt the snake's body go limp instantly.

"That's how you earn your keep," Jim nodded.

"Ooh howdy!" Billy Boy yipped. "That's a fine specimen. Whatcha say, Jim? 'Bout twelve feet?"

"Fourteen," Jim barked. "Don't go cheatin' my boy none. He did all right. For once in his life."

"How much does that get us?" Clive said, breathy and winded.

"Easy three fifty," Jim said. "Yep. Fourteen feet of alligator-eatin' invasive mother fucking python. And you caught that mother bare-handed."

Clive had. His arm felt like it was on fire, but he didn't care. That was the first compliment his father ever gave him. He waited for a chill to take the air because surely hell froze over. Clive wanted to savor the moment but knew it would spoil like milk in the sun.

"Do we gut it and dress it out here?" Clive asked.

"Nah," Jim rubbed his nose. "We gotta bag it and take it back to the Wildlife center. They measure it and count it, then write us a check."

Jim sniffled again.

"You all right?" Clive asked.

"Not sure," Jim replied. "Somethin' in the air musta gotten up my goddamn nose."

"You smell that?" Billy Boy asked, smelling the air as well.

Clive smelled it too. As he did, his heart practically leapt out of his chest. It smelled like burning rubber and musk. It smelled like a skunk. The tree line behind them rustled violently. Clive hopped off the dead snake and stood behind Jim.

The branches eight feet high in the trees behind them shook. Clive was thankful he'd just pissed in the bushes, cause only one thing in the glades stinks so bad and stands so tall, skunk ape. The creature was behind them. It moved like the wind, snapping twigs and falling branches as it ran through the woods at incredible speeds. Jim trailed it with the barrel of his gun. He knew the .22 was no good against a skunk ape, but it was all he had.

A massive hand the size of Clive's torso reached from the woods and snatched up the snake. The men jumped in surprise. If they'd have blinked, they'd have missed it. Chewing and slurping sounds echoed through the trees as Curious ol' Bob suckled the snake's head, deep-throating the serpent halfway down his throat. The men watched as the silhouette of the great skunk ape violated the snake's corpse.

Billy Boy screamed at the sight. Curious ol' Bob slowly drew out the snake, stopping only to bite off its head. Jim smacked Billy Boy on the back of his head. As the man turned to run, Jim fired a single shot into the back of Billy Boy's leg. He fell hard to the ground.

"Move!" Jim shouted at Clive.

"You son of a bitch!" Billy Boy hollered.

"But, Pa!" Clive yelled, confused.

"Run, you son of a bitch!" Jim yelled again.

Clive did as he was told, looking back briefly as the massive hand reached for Billy Boy from the woods and dragged him into the shadows.

Billy Boy dug his fingers into the loose soil, fighting for his very life. Curious ol' Bob had him good. His grip was like being crushed by a car. Billy Boy could feel the bones bending under Curious ol' Bob's fingers before snapping and breaking as it pulled him closer. He closed his eyes as he felt the creature hold him up in the air. Its fingers explored his body, gently at first. They tugged his clothes and ran along his stubbly face like warm-blooded boulders. Billy Boy felt warmth run down the front of his pants as he wet himself. He sniveled as the skunk ape pressed a cold nose into his crotch. Billy boy closed his eyes and whimpered.

Curious ol' Bob tugged at his belt. When he couldn't pull it off, he pinched the denim of his jeans and ripped them off. Billy Boy felt his tiny pecker pointing out like a finch's beak through a gnarled bush. Curious ol' Bob stroked the man's pathetic penis with growing disappointment. It ran its finger along Billy Boy's lips. He could smell rotted meat and shit under the skunk ape's fingernails.

Then Billy Boy felt something too big to be a finger brush against his cheek. It smelled like ammonia and left a warm bead of slime across his face like a snail trail. It throbbed against his skin, and Billy Boy began to cry. He didn't want to look. It took every instinct to will himself to keep his eyes shut, but curiosity won out. The shaft of Curious ol' Bob's cock was bright red with a dark purple tip, resting against his cheek. The skin was textured like a rock quarry, with herpes and warts all over the foreskin and tip. It was shaped like a dog's red rocket, with a massive scrotum dangling in the air like honey-colored oranges.

Billy Boy felt a hand along the back of his head, and it gently pressed his face into the massive cock. He struggled and fought as best he could, but the hand was too strong. His lips pressed against the warty penis, but he kept his mouth shut. The hand pushed harder, until Billy Boy could restrain no more, and the tip slid into his mouth. Pre-cum jetted across his tongue. It was a salty, viscous fluid that flooded his mouth with the foul taste of brine shrimp and butter, covered with dirt and hair.

The skunk ape's cock was like swallowing a football. It was too big for Billy Boy's mouth, but that didn't stop Curious ol' Bob. He pushed harder, breaking Billy Boy's last remaining teeth against the thick warts on his cock. The skunk ape squirmed as he felt the tight, gummy mouth work its way up and down its shaft, as Billy Boy thrashed about, struggling to work himself free.

Billy Boy's jaw snapped as it unhinged, sending a surge of pain through his body. The skunk ape continued, undeterred, wiggling its toes in ecstasy. Billy Boy scratched and clawed the shaft of the creature's cock, but it only worked to excite the beast further.

Curious ol' Bob stopped suddenly, and Billy Boy could feel the massive cock dancing in his mouth. The skunk ape clenched its whole body, as heavy streams of cum exploded in Billy Boy's mouth. The jets of foul fluids burned as they flooded his throat and jetted through his nose like white snot. Billy boy gagged, gasping for air but only breathing in the thick semen.

Curious ol' Bob pulled him off his cock and held him up to better examine his new toy. Billy Boy was broken, coughing and vomiting gallons of skunk ape seed. His jaw hung in the air, dangling in the wind as tears ran down his face. Curious ol' Bob grabbed his lower jaw and yanked free.

Blood sprayed the ground like macabre rain as Billy Boy screamed in mumbled agony. Curious ol' Bob cupped a handful of the spray and used it as lubricant, jerking himself off until he was hard again. He grabbed Billy Boy and slipped him on like a crusty sock over his freshly stiffened cock. Billy Boy could feel his skin stretch to the breaking point as he gasped for a breath of air that would not come.

Curious ol' Bob slipped in as far as he could go but was not satisfied. He pulled hard, until the skin around Billy Boy's throat and chest split open and the massive cock could easily slip deeper inside his warm body. The last few seconds of Billy Boy's life were agonizing and shameful. He thought of his wife and only wished it could have been her.

11

WINSTON WOKE TO FIND HIMSELF in a hospital bed.

"Oh, thank God!" Jennifer exclaimed. "Thank you, Mary! Thank you, Jesus!"

"What happened?" Winston blinked, finding the dim room too bright to keep his eyes open. "I feel like I got the worst hangover of my life."

"Someone spiked your drink," Freddy explained. "Got you right over to the hospital as quick as we could. You've been on fluids all night."

"Dude! You look so much better!" Dean said as he entered the room.

"How do you feel?" Jennifer asked.

"Like shit," Winston replied. "My head is killing me, and my whole body hurts."

"I'm so glad you're okay." Freddy smiled.

Jennifer smacked Freddy on the back of the head. He rocked back and forth with a twinge of hangover from his continued drinking.

"What was that for?" he asked.

"You deserve it. How could you keep drinking like that after everything that's happened? Especially to Winston!"

Winston snapped his head quickly to look at her, wanting no part in their bickering. It was then he noticed Freddy wearing sunglasses inside the hospital room.

"Did you see who did it?" Winston asked, trying to sit up.

"No," Freddy replied. "I think it was the bartender, but he was gone before the ambulance got there. It's impossible to know who did it. Doctors said you didn't get the whole dose. Just enough to knock you down for a bit."

"I guess it's my turn to really fuck this trip up." Winston shook his head.

"Not at all!" Jennifer reassured him. "That was all Freddy. We're just glad you're all right."

"Thanks," Winston replied awkwardly.

The doctors came in and checked him out. The fluids helped most of Winston's sick feeling, but he was still very weak and sore. They discharged him soon after and everyone made their way back to the SUV.

"Okay," Winston said as they got ready to pile in. "I'm sorry, but I'm not sure I can keep on with this. It's been a great trip, full of excitement and adventure, but I'm good, thanks."

"Come on, bro," Dean tried. "We've only just started!"

"Yeah." Winston side-eyed him. "That's sort of my point."

"We've already gone this far," Dean tried. "It's only a few hours till we get to Tampa. Besides, getting a flight last minute back to Cali? Are you sure you can afford that?"

"Doesn't matter. I wanna go home."

"Dean, honey," Jennifer said. "We can't make him stay."

"I'm not trying to make anyone do anything. I'm just saying we've already detoured from the plan too much as it is. Let's at least cut through Florida and see if we can't salvage something from this trip. I've already booked us a trip on an airboat and a campsite for the night. Come on, Winston, Freddy told me you love camping."

"I'm sure he did," Winston looked at Freddy, betrayed.

"Look, if you want to go, you can book yourself a flight for tomorrow or the day after in Tampa. Let's not ruin the trip for everyone else. I promise, the worst is already behind us."

"Okay," Winston rolled his eyes and looked up for God to strike him down for saying it.

"That's it!" Dean smiled. "What's the worst that could happen?"

———————————————▶

Dean regretted the airboat tour as soon as they'd arrived. It was not like the website advertised. It showed the building as bright and friendly, with droves of tourists petting baby alligators and laughing as their boats made sharp turns this way and that. The building was red, that much was the same, but everything else about it was a stark contrast of what was advertised.

The place looked like an abandoned barn, decrepit with moldy siding and a rusted tin roof. The boats took on a great deal of water, with dark green algae caking their sides. The air smelled musty and a lot like dead fish. The bright orange paint flaked off, revealing more rust and crumbling metal around the fans and benches.

Worse, the man who greeted them had only four teeth and whistled when he spoke. His arms and legs were purple with dark red and brown splotches underneath a thin carpet of white hair. The hair on the rest of his body more than made up for the little hair left on his head.

"Ya'll here for the tour?" he said, tipping his musty ball cap at them.

"I think so," Dean offered a smile at his group.

"You gotta be fucking kidding," Jennifer said.

"It can't be that bad," Dean replied.

"Yes, it can," Freddy added. "Have you ever seen *Deliverance?* The second I hear banjos, I'm out."

"I kind of agree with Freddy on this one," Winston shook his head. "It looks sketchy."

"What's that supposed to mean?" asked the crotchety old man.

"Look," Dean offered a handshake to the old man, who coldly rejected it. "I don't know what's going on here, but this doesn't look anything like the website."

"Oh," the old man clapped and laughed. "That ol' thing. Had my nephew do it up for me. Looks great don't it?"

"Online it does," Dean replied. "But this, this looks nothing like what you advertised."

"You ain't from 'round here, are you?"

"No."

"See, this is an Everglades tour. This buildin' here been in my family since my great granddaddy. We done what we can to keep it up. Even installed a real toilet myself. Back a few years ago. But this time here is the off-season. We don't get much of you touristy types much in the summer time on account of the heat and hurricanes."

"Okay, but that doesn't explain why the building looks like shit here and looks brand new on the website."

"I dunno, I think this place looks fine to me."

"It doesn't look like you've seen a tourist since the nineteen-hundreds."

"All tickets are nonrefundable. You either take the tour, or ya get on."

Dean looked back at the group.

"You can't be serious," Jennifer scolded.

"We're already here," Dean tried.

"Already here, my ass!"

"You just want your money's worth," Freddy shook his head.

"I'll sit this one out," Winston said. "I've seen this movie. The black guy dies first."

"Dude, come on, guys!" Dean pleaded as they walked back to the car. "We don't have to go inside, just the airboat ride. It's what, an hour out of your lives? Come on! Bro, I paid for this shit!"

"Fine," Jennifer rolled her eyes. "But this shit better not kill me, 'cause I will haunt your ass for the rest of your life."

"What if it kills me too?" Dean asked.

"Then you will find out what Hell really is."

With Jennifer on board, Freddy and Winston caved, and they all followed the old man to the boats.

"My name's Curtis," he introduced. "Watch yer step, this dock's older than dirt."

Nervously, they stepped on the old dock. The wood planks creaked and shifted under each delicate step they took. The water below was murky and brown. Gnats and mosquitoes buzzed through the air like clouds of pestilence as they waited for Curtis to finish fueling the fan.

"Anyone get any reception out here?" Freddy asked, waving his phone in the air, trying to find a signal.

"Yep," Dean said pulling out his phone. "Dude, I got the best plan there is. The sales guy at the place said I could post a selfie on Mount Everest, it's so good. Once we get going, I dunno how much you'll need your phone, though."

"Yeah, I just wanted to post one last picture of myself before I die."

They piled onto the long airboat. There were three benches, two in the front that could seat four people, and one in the back by the fan for the driver. The benches were little more than lawn furniture held down by L-brackets and JB Weld. It did little to put the group at ease as they sat down and felt the benches shift left and right.

Curtis handed them each a pair of headphones with microphones. Freddy placed it to his nose and regretted it immediately. It stank of stagnant water and sweat.

"You might wanna keep those on," Curtis said to Freddy, taking his place in the driver seat. "This thing gets pretty loud."

"What about life preservers?" Winston asked.

"What?" Curtis asked as he fired up the engine.

He wasn't kidding. The fan motor was like sitting next to a plane engine at high rev. The airboat lurched forward as he put it in gear and gunned it out of the docks. Everyone grabbed onto whatever they could for dear life. The wind whipped across their faces, stinging them with bugs and brown water spray as they splashed on. The headphones rang with static as Curtis turned on the radio function

"Good afternoon," Curtis said into a microphone on his headset. "And welcome to Curtis Tucker's Everglades Airboat Tour. Please don't feed the wildlife, and keep your hands, fingers, and toes inside the boat at all times."

They zoomed through the brown waters at nearly thirty miles an hour. Only Jennifer and Freddy wore sunglasses, while Dean and Winston felt the wind stinging their eyes.

"What you see up here," Curtis continued his commentary, "are what we call sawgrass. The leaves have sharp serrated edges like saw blades. You don't wanna go runnin' through these bushes, or it'll be some bad times.

"You'll also see some cattails up in here. They look like little corn dogs we give the tourists around November. Sure, you could eat 'em, but they ain't gonna taste no good."

"Why do we have to use an airboat along here?" Freddy asked. "Why not just use a regular boat that's a little quieter?"

"You see," Curtis explained as he slowed the boat down, "these waters look deep, but don't be fooled. That's about as shallow as a bathtub. Plus, the flat bottom is good for crunching cattails and not killin' any gators."

"There's gators out here?" Jennifer asked, startled.

"Whooh girl!" Curtis laughed. "You see standin' water, you can bet your knickers that they got a gator in it. Canals, ponds, swimmin' pools, you name it. See, you run over a gator with a normal propeller and it ruins ya blades. You hit one with one of these, and you just glide right over."

"Wouldn't that hurt them?" Winston asked.

"I never asked." Curtis laughed some more. "Too busy gettin' the hell out their way."

Curtis stopped his boat around a small bunch of mangroves.

"See that flat land up there?" He pointed out an indentation in the tall grasses. "That there is a gator trail. Most likely she got some eggs up in there. You never wanna go near one of them trails. Mama gators are ornery things when they mad."

"What's that over there?" Freddy asked, pointing to the other side of the boat.

It was another indentation, only this was too big for an alligator. Branches and trees were knocked down to clear a path into a densely wooded area.

"Only thing worse than gators out here in the glades," Curtis said, the humor in his voice lost. "Skunk ape. Curious ol' Bob, as us locals like to call him."

"Why's he called Curious?" Dean asked. "And what's a skunk ape?"

"He's like a sasquatch . . ." Curtis tried to find the right words. "You know? Bigfoot. Only skunk apes are far more ornery, and they stink to high heaven like a skunk. The name says it all. They call him Curious ol' Bob 'cause he takes a likin' to people of both kinds, the men and the ladies. He's been known for attacking men and women in a rather . . . well, I'd prefer not to talk about it too much. Let's just say he's about the only skunk ape I know of without fear of people. You smell that skunk smell, you best go runnin', 'cause you can't out-hide no skunk ape."

12

"WHY THE HELL YA SHOOT him for?" Clive asked Jim as they made it back to the main trail.

"That fucker caught the damn thing's attention," Jim replied, his hands on his knees as he struggled to catch his breath. "I got my bad knee. I can't run like I used to. When shit hits the fan, you don't gotta be the fastest, only beat the slowest. Survival. We lived. He died. Or should I leave you next time?"

"No! I thought he was your friend?"

"What good are friends when you're dead? Friends come and go. I'd be more upset if that wife of his could fit through her front door. She gonna be madder than a bear restin' his nut sack on an ant hill."

"What we gonna do?"

"We ain't gonna do nothin'. We're goin' home. I'ma call Fish and Wildlife and tell 'em no luck."

"Won't they know somethin's wrong when Billy Boy doesn't come home?"

"They don't know about Billy Boy. He's got a felony for cookin' meth. He's not even supposed to be huntin' them snakes."

"Don't you think his wife might think we done somethin'?"

"That fat bitch might just think he ran off to find somethin' younger and thinner. You will not say shit to nobody. Do you understand me, boy?"

Clive swallowed hard. He'd just done his father proud. He couldn't disappoint him now. Clive nodded his head yes.

"Say it," Jim barked.

"I won't say nothin' to nobody," Clive promised.

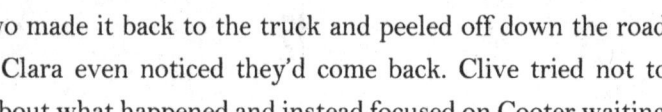

The two made it back to the truck and peeled off down the road before Clara even noticed they'd come back. Clive tried not to think about what happened and instead focused on Cooter waiting back in the shed. They pulled up to the house and got out of the truck. Clive waited for Pa to go inside before he made his way back to the shed.

Abigail grabbed her brother's crotch from behind. Clive jumped in surprise.

"Got your dick!" Abigail laughed.

"Why the hell you gone and done that?" Clive stammered, trying to regain his composure.

"What crawled up your butt?" she asked

"Nothin', frog face. Just, I got a lot on my mind. That's all."

"Ha! You think of nothin' but titties and food. What the hell could you have on your mind?"

"Nothin'!"

"Don't sound like nothin'."

"Leave it alone!"

"Motherfucker, I know when you up to no good. I can sense it."

"I'm not up to anything."

"So how was snake huntin'?"

"Didn't catch nothin'."

"Not surprised. You couldn't catch a cold if someone sneezed it on you. What happened the other night?"

"Nothin'."

"You said that, already! Why did Pa come home by himself? Why did you walk home?"

"I got lost."

"You find Curious ol' Bob?"

"Nah."

"'Cause you know how ol' Bob just loves you. He thinks you smell nice."

"Yeah, 'cause you smell like the devil's dick."

"If that was true, it'd be your fault."

"I didn't see Curious ol' Bob, all right?"

"What did you see?"

"I was bit by a hog last night, then by a snake today."

"I thought you said you didn't find anything?"

"We didn't. It got away."

"Where'd you get bit?"

"You don't see this blood on my arm?"

"I didn't know what it was. How big was the hog?"

"It was big, but there were a bunch."

"How many?"

"Eight of 'em."

"Eight? Eight hogs?"

"Yep."

"And the snake?"

"Was longer than Pa's truck! He said sixteen feet."

"You lying sack a shit!"

"I ain't lyin'!"

"You can't count past five. All you know it was one little piglet and you just ran off scared of your own dick."

Clive pulled off his shirt and showed her the bite marks.

"See?" Clive said, pressing his shoulder in her face.

"Damn!" Abigail oohed and aahed. "Must have been a big one! You didn't get Ma to come clean this up?"

"Not yet. I didn't have no time last night, and we just got back."

"Why were you fixin' the henhouse?"

"'Cause I wanted to fix it and make up to Pa for last night."

"Suspicious."

"'Cause I'm doin' my chores?"

"Exactly!"

"I ain't got time for this."

"You must have done somethin' else real bad."

"Nothin'!"

"Will you stop sayin' 'nothin'!"

"I won't 'cause it's the truth!"

"I heard you did."

"If you heard, why you askin'?"

"'Cause I wanna hear you say it."

"I ain't gonna."

"Last night ya gave Pa his gun with no bullets in it!"

"Shut up!"

"If Pa didn't have no bullets in his pocket like he always does, he might have had a bite like you. Think how mad Pa might be then!"

"I don't wanna."

"Where ya goin'?"

"I wanna clean out the damn shed."

"Suspicious!"

"Ain't nothin' suspicious about cleanin'."

"It is when ya don't want me followin' ya!"

"'Cause I got shit to do."

"I wanna see."

"See what?"

"What you gotta 'clean up.'"

"No!"

Abigail turned and ran toward the shed. Clive tried to catch her but was too late. Abigail stepped inside, her eyes adjusting to the darkness. Something moved in the shadows. She went to look for it, but it was gone. Abigail squatted, thinking it may have been a coon or a rat.

Something moved again. It was too big to be a coon. Then she saw it. The gray-fleshed monster nested under the workbench. Its lips peeled back in a fierce growl, showing off its three needle-like fangs. Abigail went to scream, but Clive grabbed her from behind, putting his hand over her mouth. He'd shut her up just in time.

"I told you not to come in here," Clive whispered in her ear. "Cooter ain't gonna hurt you. Now when I let you go, you better not scream. Promise?"

Abigail nodded, her wide eyes focused on Cooter. Clive released his grip and let her go.

"What the hell is that?" Abigail asked.

"That's my new dog!" Clive said proudly. "I found her last night. Named her Cooter."

"How do you know it's a her?"

"I just figured since she ain't got no nuts she might be a girl. That's why I went with Cooter. It could go either way, I suppose, kinda like Bobby Joe, or Bobby Jo."

"I don't think that's no dog."

"Sure she is! Look at them big ol' puppy dog eyes!"

Clive bent down and scratched behind Cooter's ear, right in the kick spot.

"Why ain't she got no hair then?" Abigail asked, closing the shed doors behind her.

"I dunno. Figured she was born that way."

"You know Pa ain't gonna like this none. He don't like regular dogs. I ain't gonna lie, she's uglier than sin."

"No, she ain't! You take that back!"

"She gots no hair, Clive! And her skin is all sweaty. She looks like a ball sack!"

"Yer face looks like a frog and we still feed you and dress you nice."

"What are you gonna do with her?"

"I wanna keep her."

"You know you can't."

"Why not?"

"'Cause those teeth. Is she the one who ate all Ma's chickens?"

"Ya can't prove nothin'."

"Clive, look at her teeth. Them's the same teeth that bled all them chickens."

"She didn't mean to!"

"And a panther don't mean no harm shakin' yer hand, but his claws still cut you good."

"Abigail, I ain't never asked you for nothin' in your life."

"Except all them times you asked me to suck yer dick."

"That's nothin'. I never asked to borrow no money, no toys, nothin'. I never asked you for no favors. Help me, I wanna find somewhere we can keep Cooter, so Pa don't see."

"Okay. I'll help. But you owe me big time. I gotta get ready for lunch at the restaurant soon. I promise not to say nothin'."

Clive spat in his hand and presented it to Abigail. She rolled her eyes and spat in hers, then shook his hand. It was a promise signed with DNA. She helped her brother finish the henhouse and cleaned up for the lunch rush. They said nothing about Cooter, but neither could help but pass a glance at the shed. Cooter was an ugly bitch, but she made Clive happy. Clive wasn't the brightest crayon in the box, but he was still her brother, and if Cooter made him happy, she would help him as best she could.

Cooter paced back and forth in the shed, peeking through the cracked siding. She watched as Clive and his sister fixed the henhouse. Cooter felt a rumble in her stomach that turned like stones. She was hungry. She walked to the other side of the shed, pressing her nose to the cracks for a scent of anything good enough to eat.

It didn't take long. An iguana climbed down a tall pine tree and sat on the gravel, sunning itself in the hot Florida sun. Cooter licked her lips and pressed harder against the planks. She felt them shift suddenly as the dry rotted wood slid right over the nail heads. With her hands, she gently pushed the boards free, just enough so she could fit through and not startle the lizard. She hunched low to the ground, staying downwind and out of the lizard's line of sight.

As Cooter was about to pounce, the iguana turned its head and saw her. It dashed back into the woods, and Cooter ran, chasing after it.

13

THE AIRBOATS WEREN'T A TOTAL wash. The ride was fun, and the creepy-as-hell tour guide only added to the trip's mystique. By the time they'd finished, it was already past three in the afternoon and everyone was starving.

"Know anywhere good to eat?" Dean asked Curtis.

"Sure," Curtis said, spitting over the side of the airboat as he fiddled with the motor. "This place right up the street, the Red Crab. It's authentic Florida cracker cookin'."

"Cracker cooking?" Freddy asked.

"That's right," Curtis replied. "Old time word for Florida folks. Back in the day, when people got around with horse and buggy, Florida riders would use a whip to drive 'em. They called 'em crackers, after the whip sound."

"See?" Winston said to Freddy. "You even learned something new today."

"We're talking again?" Freddy asked.

"No," Winston shrugged. "Just hungry like everyone else."

"Sounds good." Dean went to shake Curtis's hand.

Curtis looked him over and went back to work on his motor.

"Thanks," Dean said, shaking his head.

"Where you folks plannin' on sleepin'?" Curtis asked.

"We rented a campsite a few miles west of here," Dean replied.

"Campsite?"

"Yeah, we got tents and stuff like that."

"I'm not sure that's such a great idea."

"Why's that?"

"You 'member that path in the grass, the one Curious ol' Bob made?"

"Yeah?"

"Ain't no one seen him this far south in years. Him comin' out is no good sign. If I was you, I'd turn around and find a nice, clean motel to hunker down in for the night."

"Thanks, bro, but we kinda wanted a romantic night under the stars."

"Suit yourself. None of my business should a skunk ape sneak up from the water at night and getcha."

"Yeah. All right, thanks."

Dean nodded and pinched his lips. Clearly the man was crazy, or superstitious. Dean had plans, and things were already in motion. No one would get in his way, not Freddy and Winston's bullshit, and definitely not some crotchety old man.

"Where're we eating?" Freddy asked back at the car.

"Said there was a local place right up the street." Dean pointed in the direction. "Should be on our way to the campsite."

"I'm starving," Jennifer complained.

"We all are," Freddy said as he hopped in the back seat after Winston.

Dean rolled his eyes as he waited for everyone to get in and situated before taking off.

←——————————————→

Curtis was right; it wasn't far. The building was hard to miss. A big picture of a smiling red crab was painted on the sign, and the words 'Established in 1902' underneath the restaurant's name, The Red Crab. The siding was painted bright blue, while the skirting around the stilts that lifted the building off the ground were painted red. From the parking area, they could see the large screened-in patio that wrapped around the left side of the building.

"This is kinda cute," Dean offered his encouragement.

"Smells like a dead canal," Freddy replied.

"Is it even safe to eat here?" Winston asked.

"Should be fine," Dean shrugged.

"I don't care," Jennifer said, hopping out of the car. "I'm starving."

Inside was a wide-open dining room with coolers against the back wall filled with glass-bottled sodas and beer of all kinds. The dining room looked as if a flea market threw up in it. None of the tables, benches, or chairs matched. Doilies were used instead of tablecloths. The ceiling was littered with burns and beer bottles and a hodgepodge of random lanterns. It was hardly a five-star dining room, but hopefully the food would be much better.

"Hey y'all!" greeted a lanky young blond. "Name's Abigail. Menus on the table, drinks are self-service so keep your bottles in the milk crates on y'alls table when ya finish 'em. Have a seat wherever you like. I'll be with you in a few."

Abigail smiled and walked back toward the kitchen.

"You guys wanna sit on the patio?" Dean asked

"Maybe," Freddy replied, fanning himself with his hand. "I was hoping this place had AC, but nope."

"Maybe it'll be breezy outside," Dean said. "Let's grab some beers first."

They went to the coolers, grabbed a few bottles, and sat down on the wicker furniture with a parquet table top on the screened in patio. Ceiling fans spun slowly above them with long dusty tails dragging through the air like ghosts.

"Dude, at least they have good beer," Dean said, taking his seat.

"How the hell do you guys drink IPAs?" Freddy asked both Dean and Winston. "It tastes like piss."

"How do you know what piss tastes like?" Dean smiled.

"It's just so damn bitter," Freddy sneered.

"Nah," Dean waved him off. "It's just the hops. You get all kinds of floral notes, and it's super crisp. It's like not drinking light beer. You get all this flavor."

"Piss flavor."

"Are we the only people in this whole place?" Jennifer asked.

"We were the only car out front," Dean replied, sipping his bottle.

"You don't think that's a little bit weird?"

"Don't worry, babe. We're in the middle of nowhere, and it's between rushes. I don't think they get a lot of tourists this time of year."

"Sure don't," Abigail said as she pulled out a pencil and pad. "This time of year's usually still too hot for people traveling. Where y'all from?"

"California," Dean replied.

"Oh, that's nice!" Abigail nodded. "Just on vacation in our sunshine state?"

"Pretty much," Dean smiled. "Road trip from Key West all the way back to Cali."

"Sounds pretty nice! We don't get out of town a whole lot. The restaurant is a full-time thing for the family, ya know what I mean? So whatcha all havin'?"

"I didn't even look at the menu yet," Freddy said, exasperated.

"I'll have the soft-shell crab sandwich," Winston said, his nose in the menu.

"Burger and fries." Jennifer pointed.

"You're not gonna try anything different?" Dean asked.

"No." Jennifer shook her head.

"We're on vacation," Dean insisted. "We should be trying all kinds of local deliciousness!"

"Or, no." Jennifer forced a smiled.

"I'll try the frog legs," Dean rolled his eyes and handed the menu to Abigail.

"I'll do the alligator basket," Freddy said, excited.

"Put that right in for you guys!" Abigail winked and walked off toward the back.

"What's the plan after this?" Winston asked.

"We eat," Dean said, sipping his beer. "Then we go about three or four miles west to the park. Check in at the reservation area, then pitch camp."

"As long as we get there before dark," Jennifer said.

"I'm surprised you agreed to go camping," Freddy laughed.

"What's that supposed to mean?" Jennifer glared at her brother.

"I mean, you're not exactly the outdoorsy type."

"And look at you, Mr. 'I can't start a gas grill with a lighter.'"

"That's different, all right? Setting fire to wood is different when you don't have the damn valve-thing you gotta turn on first. Wood is always turned on."

"So punny." Winston shook his head.

"You know it," Freddy smiled.

Freddy put his hand on Winston's thigh, but Winston quickly moved over. The table grew quiet as Jennifer and Dean felt the awkwardness like a dead body over their shoulders.

"Sorry," Freddy said.

Winston didn't reply and, instead, sipped his beer.

"So," Dean said abruptly, trying to break up the tension. "There's a bunch of stuff to do at the campsite. They have kayaking, nature trails, nature, stuff like that."

Freddy tuned Dean out. He wanted to make it up to Winston. He wanted them to get past this. Things were still too fresh. Maybe that night they could go for a walk and talk things out.

"I gotta pee," Freddy said as he got up from the table.

He followed the signs to the restroom and saw Abigail talking to a guy out front. He was just as tall and lanky, possibly her brother by the looks of it. His hands were covered in blisters, his dark blond hair was all knotted, and his overalls were stained with what looked like blood.

"She got out," the guy said. "We gotta find her!"

"Clive!" Abigail shouted. "We got customers. Keep your damn voice down!"

"She's gonna kill some more if we don't find her," Clive whispered loudly.

"Then you better go after her before Pa finds out. You're lucky he had to go to the supply store."

"When he gets home, just keep him distracted."

Clive ran off and Abigail turned back toward the front door. Freddy went quickly into the bathroom and out of sight just in time as she came back in.

What were they talking about? Freddy thought to himself. He didn't like the sound of it, and the pornography plastering the walls didn't help his gut feeling get any better.

14

AFTER SOME SERIOUS CHASING UP and down the canal, Cooter finally caught the lizard, but it didn't go down without a fight. It whipped its tail hard across her face, which only angered her further. In a fit of rage, Cooter leaped on top of the reptile, bared down her claws, and bit it just behind the skull. Her fangs almost pierced clean through the other side, but she withdrew them and suckled on the lizard's gushing wound. She could feel the animal's struggles begin to wane as the body slowly went limp and cold. In minutes, it was all over.

Cooter dropped the carcass from her mouth and licked her lips. Iguanas made for good snacks, but she was still hungry. She sniffed the air, her hypersensitive nose detecting something bright and metallic in the distance. Blood. Cooter chased after it without hesitation. It wasn't far, but the dense brush and shallow-water marshes made any travel much more grueling.

Swarms of mosquitoes buzzed around her in a cloud of hypodermic needles itching for a bite. They landed on her back, neck, and ears, poking around for the softest flesh they might steal a drink of blood from. Cooter shook and scratched, but the cloud was too much. Her skin grew inflamed where they bit her, burning and itching until she gave a yelp in pain.

Cooter growled and dove into a nearby canal, drowning those that didn't fly away in time. She walked up the bank and jumped in a puddle of mud, shaking and rolling around so her whole body was caked in the brown goo. Sufficiently coated, the bugs couldn't get through. Cooter panted, smiling as the mosquitoes tried and failed.

Mud covered, she went back into the brush in search of that sweet scent of blood. She came to a clearing and was overcome by a noxious smell. Sniffing the air, Cooter's nose tickled with the scent of skunk, that rotted cabbage and burnt tire stink that soaked into your skin for days. It made her eyes water and her nose runny, but the smell of blood only made her hungrier.

What she found was a bear impaled to a tree. The bear's feet dangled three feet off the ground, dripping with blood welling from a wound in its chest. A branch pierced its back and shot through its chest, as if the body was hung there for safekeeping. Its head was turned at an unnatural angle, the bones in its neck protruding from its gore-stained fur.

Blood pooled at the bear's feet, dripping into a puddle of crimson mud beneath it. Cooter went to sniff the bear, but the smell of skunk overpowered everything else. She bit the animal's foot, lapping up what blood was left as she tried not to smell the air.

As she did, something moved in the brush behind her. It was a loud snap as twigs broke under heavy weight. Cooter stopped eating and looked quickly in that direction. Her heart was racing, her skin alive with goosebumps under the mud. She reared her back and shoulders to appear bigger, baring her teeth with a low growl.

Branches and twigs broke several feet in the air. Whatever this was, it was big. Before Cooter even saw it, she darted back into the brush again, running as fast as her legs could carry her. She didn't stop, leaping over fallen logs and ducking under low branches.

It wasn't until she'd come to a barbed wire fence overlooking a wide-open pasture that she finally stopped. It was a farm, full of cows, goats, and chickens lazily grazing in the safety of the barbed wire fence. Cooter looked at the cows greedily. She'd only sipped a few tablespoons of bear blood, and the iguana only made her hungrier.

With the danger behind her, Cooter turned her attention to the animals. The cows' thick, massive necks made her mouth water, while the thought of chickens and goats made her stomach grumble with hunger. She tried to push her way between the wire but yelped in surprise as one of the barbs scratched her.

Cooter was no quitter. She looked around and saw a tree branch dangling over the fence. It didn't take her long to get to the top, her raccoon-like hands and thumbs grabbing the tree bark with skilled dexterity. The overhanging branch was more than sixteen feet off the ground. It was a hell of a drop, but Cooter wasn't deterred. She leapt from the branch, the webbing between her arms and sides catching air like a sugar glider as she gracefully swooped through the air and back onto all fours.

Crouching just below the tall grass, Cooter prowled the pastures like a panther, eyeing the henhouse closest to her. She stepped into the clearing, stalking silently with her body close to the ground. The hens were none the wiser, casually pecking and clucking to their hearts' content. By the time they'd noticed Cooter, it was too late. She'd sprung on them, and in just a few seconds, bit, clawed, and strangled all the chickens in the henhouse before a single fowl could squawk or screech for help.

White and brown blood-stained feathers blanketed the chicken coop as Cooter fed at her leisure, taking shade in the henhouse from the scorching afternoon sun. She'd about finished them off when a goat happened upon the carnage. At the sight of blood, it bleated out, crying for help as the other animals fled the scene. Cooter shot out of the henhouse, knowing all too well trouble often followed cries for help. The goat that cried out froze at the sight of her and fell over to one side, its body stiff as a board.

Cooter jumped back in surprise, but curiosity drew her closer. She'd never seen an animal faint before. She smelled its rear, then its belly and mouth. It was still breathing but didn't move as she nudged it with her nose. Not one to turn down an easy meal, she bit down on the animal's neck, holding it down with her arms as it shot back to life. It bleated louder, until Cooter squeezed against its windpipe, shushing the baby goat until its body went limp in her mouth.

As she began to feed, a gunshot sounded not far off. Dirt exploded inches beside her. She looked up to where the sound came from. It was a man, potbellied and shirtless, running toward her, trying to reload his break-action shotgun.

Cooter hissed and ran toward the chicken coop. The man snapped the barrels back into place and took aim, his drunken hands wavering as he struggled to get a bead on her. His sweaty finger squeezed the trigger, taking out the hinges on the coop and missing Cooter completely. Cooter made it to the top of the coop, hissed at the man, and unfolded the membrane under her arms.

With only a few feet of runway, Cooter dashed off and leapt into the air, gliding with just enough wind beneath her to swoop on top of the man with the gun. She came down hard, digging her claws into his pink flesh like over-ripened fruit. He shouted at her, dropping his gun in surprise. Cooter clawed his face and body, her nails digging right through to the bone.

The man tried to fight, swinging his arms wildly, but Cooter was stronger than her thin frame suggested, and she restrained him easily. She opened her mouth and bit down hard on the man's throat. His screams faded to a wet, slurping sound as his windpipe flooded with blood. It sprayed jets of red as she released his neck, showering her with his hot delicious crimson waters. She licked her face before pressing her lips to the wound welling with gore.

The man's body went cold in her arms. Cooter suckled his neck until there was nothing left. He was sweeter than anything she'd ever tasted, and his blood was thick and fatty as a slug. Once she'd bled him dry, she released him and licked herself clean.

"Dad?" someone called in the distance.

More strangers, more people. Cooter needed to get away. She ran as fast as her legs could carry her, spreading her arms and unfurling the membrane under them. With the faintest breeze, she leapt, catching the wind, and glided into the air. All the little boy saw was his father, cold and dead on the ground, and the monster that killed him leaping over the fence.

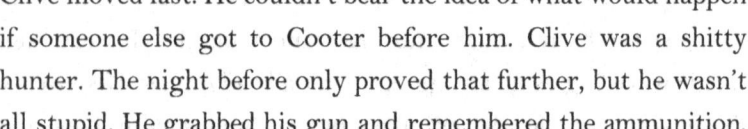

Clive moved fast. He couldn't bear the idea of what would happen if someone else got to Cooter before him. Clive was a shitty hunter. The night before only proved that further, but he wasn't all stupid. He grabbed his gun and remembered the ammunition. He stuffed his pockets till they overflowed with brass and took off into the Everglades.

Running through the brush, he thought about where Cooter could have gone. There was plenty of wildlife for her to feed on in the glades, but it would take him days to find her. He thought more while jumping fallen logs and ducking under and around low hanging branches. Running barefoot made him feel more confident, like he was one with the earth in the art of tracking.

Though his art was more of a fingerpainting, he managed to come across the stink of skunk musk. Clive followed it and saw the bear hanging on a tree with a broken neck. The smell was almost unbearable, burning his nose and eyes, but the sight of a bear with a broken neck was too much to ignore. It meant only one thing, Curious ol' Bob. Clive's skin went clammy and his heart raced.

Clive ran faster than that time an alligator chased him, even with a rifle slung over his shoulder bouncing into every tangled branch he came across. By the time he came to the farm, the police were already there. It was too far away to see with the naked eye, so he peeked through his rifle scope, careful to keep his finger off the trigger.

Police snapped pictures of the crime scene. It was his family's neighbor, Diabetus Dave, lying dead on the ground. He was a simple man, a God-fearing Christian who suffered a bit of gluttony with the pies his wife always made. Soon, his appetite left him with amputated toes and fingers, and by the looks of things, right into the jaws of Clive's beloved Cooter. It had to be her. The henhouse was in shambles, with bloody feathers all over, like an exploded pillow.

Wherever she was, she'd been long gone. The sun was beginning to set, but Clive refused to give up, not until he found her.

15

"WE SHOULDN'T STAY LONG." FREDDY quickly took his seat at the table as everyone dug into their food.

"What do you mean?" Dean asked with a mouth full of frog legs.

"There's some weird shit going on," Freddy said.

"Then sit down and eat so we can leave!" Jennifer shouted.

Freddy rolled his eyes and sat down.

"What happened?" Winston asked.

"I just heard our waitress talking to some guy outside," Freddy whispered to the group. "He was covered in mud or something—it looked like blood—and they were talking about someone killing people."

"That's weird," Winston gasped.

"Bro, really? You sure that's what they were talking about?" Dean asked, biting into another frog thigh.

"I'm serious!" Freddy raised his voice.

"How you folks doing?" Abigail said, patting Dean's back in greeting.

"Fine," Freddy said quickly.

"If y'all need anything, just holler!" Abigail smiled and left them alone outside.

"Are you sure?" Dean smiled as he shook his head.

"Why would they be talking about killing people?" Jennifer asked. "This is just a restaurant. If they killed people, they'd never get customers."

"You see any customers right now?" Freddy asked.

"There weren't any customers at the airboat place either," Winston added.

"Look, dude," Dean polished off the bottle of beer and continued, "I get it. You guys are uncomfortable and ya wanna go. Let's just get to the campsite, get through the night, and come up with a plan tomorrow."

"It's not about that!" Freddy snapped back.

"Bro, I told you already," Dean replied calmly, "we've been planning this trip for a long time. It's already started off on the wrong foot. Let's all relax, calm down, enjoy our night out in the wild, and revisit this tomorrow. I don't think a girl as sweet and virginal as our waitress could possibly be connected with some murderer. Just look at her! I don't think she could even say 'boob' without blushing."

"You have a track record of fucking shit up for the rest of us," Jennifer told her brother. "You know exactly what I'm talking about, or do I have to bring it up in front of God and everyone? Not you, Winston. This is something else."

Freddy said nothing and ate his alligator tenders in silence. No one wanted to believe him, not even his sister. It was bullshit for her to bring that up again. The dig did more than just anger him; it hurt.

Winston was looking at him, confused by what Jennifer was talking about. Freddy couldn't look at him. He couldn't let him see just how angry he really was. Freddy began to second-guess himself. Maybe Dean was right. Maybe he hadn't heard what he thought he did. One thing he did know was that he hoped he'd just imagined the whole thing.

←—————————————→

The peak temperature in California might be the same as Florida, but the nights in the Sunshine State never seemed to cool down. And that oppressive humidity meant all the sweat that poured out of them did absolutely nothing to cool them down.

The campsite wasn't exactly like the brochure. There were places for RV hookups and power outlets at each campsite, but it wasn't the Everglades oasis the pictures made it out to be. The gently flowing rivers were algae infested runoff canals. The learning center was little more than a taxidermy exhibit, and a bad one at that. The animals looked mangy and cross-eyed, with weird half smiles contorted in unnatural angles.

Even the camping spot they'd been assigned wasn't what Dean expected. He was told, "A night of roughing it in grassy fields under a starry night." What they got was a gravel driveway and a steel drum fire pit underneath a pinewood forest. Judging by the overcast sky and the dense forest canopy, there would be no starry night for them.

As the sun began to set, Dean threw some blocks of firewood he'd purchased at the ranger station entrance into the stumpy metal drum and tried getting a fire going. The wood was wet. Despite the lighter fluid he sprayed over it and the copious amount of matches he'd thrown, it just didn't want to light.

"We need better wood," Winston tried to help as the sun began its descent.

"This is what we've got," Dean sneered as he stuffed pine needles and some of the toilet paper they'd brought under the logs for kindling.

"If the wood is wet," Winston said. "Then it doesn't matter how much toilet paper you light on fire, it's not going to catch right away. You need fresh, dry wood to burn so you can dry out the wet stuff."

"Bro . . . I got this." Dean threw a side-glance at Winston.

Winston shook his head and sat back in his folding chair. Jennifer waited by the fire pit with a lap full of s'mores supplies. Impatient, she began eating the marshmallows. Dean smacked the back of his neck.

"Fucking bugs!" he grunted.

"I told you." Jennifer bobbed her head side to side, mouthing a big fluffy marshmallow. "Put on some bug spray."

"I don't want any of that DDT shit on me!" Dean sneered, slapping his arm as another bug bit him. "Fuck!"

"Fine." Jennifer shrugged.

"I'm gonna go for a walk," Winston said, going to the back of the SUV for a flashlight. "See if I can get some dry firewood, maybe."

"I'll go with you," Freddy volunteered.

"I'm fine by myself." Winston crossed his arms.

"It's getting late," Dean said, taking a break from his fire starting. "You don't wanna be alone in the woods after dark."

"Fine," Winston rolled his eyes. "As if I'm not a grown-ass man."

"Honey, my phone's not working. You have any service?" Jennifer asked while Freddy grabbed a light for himself.

"Dude," Dean got up and handed her his phone. "I have that amazing unlimited plan. It's like, the best service on the planet. I've gone out of my way to find places it can't get reception, and I've never found one."

Freddy found a lantern in the back of the SUV and clicked it twice so the light wasn't blinding bright, just enough for them to see where they were going.

"Be safe, you two," Jennifer said, her glance focused on the phone.

←——————————————→

Freddy could feel the tension building with every step. They'd been walking the trail nearly fifteen minutes. Neither of them spoke.

"So," Freddy began nervously, "what do you think of Florida?"

"Humid as fuck," Winston replied coldly.

"How do we know the wood we're gonna find is dry?"

"You touch it."

"No reason to be sarcastic."

"No, that was just a dumb question."

"There are no dumb questions."

"Only dumb people."

"How many times to I have to say I'm sorry?"

"Once, and honestly. That might be good enough."

"I did apologize!"

"Yeah, while you were drunk with another man's hand around your dick."

"And all day after that! It's not like that."

"Then what the fuck is it like?!"

"I was—"

"Drunk. Yeah, I got that. But that doesn't take away how much it fucking hurts."

"This silent treatment sucks, too. You didn't speak to me all day, until back at the crab shack place."

"You say 'murderous white folk' around a gay black dude and his spidey senses tingle."

"I'm sorry, Winston. Honest to God. I don't know what came over me back in the Keys. I fucked up. I know I did."

"All right."

"All right?"

"Yeah."

"What do we do now?"

"Find some goddamn wood."

"Are we cool now?"

"No."

"What the fuck?"

"You cheated on me, Freddy. Yes, the apology helps, but that doesn't change the fact that it happened. I'm going to need more time. Remember when I said that the first time? You know, after you proposed to me?"

"I love you."

"I know you do. But we've only been dating for a short time. I know I'm your first out-of-the-closet boyfriend, but six months isn't enough time for a marriage proposal."

"So, you don't love me back?"

"I didn't say that."

"You also didn't say it back."

"No, you are not turning this around on me. I didn't say it because it's too fucking soon. Yes, I have feelings for you. Yes, it's probably love. But I don't say that to just any random person I'm seeing. I want it to be real. I want it to mean something."

"I mean it every time I say it."

"I know you do. I just want to mean it when I say it back."

"Does that mean you want to work this out?"

"Seeing you with another man hurt me more than I'd expected. I mean, yeah, I've been cheated on before, and it sucked then, too, but this hurt more than the other time. I guess I do have stronger feelings for you than I admitted before."

"Then I go and fuck that up."

"See? Now we're on the same page again."

"At least there's that."

They kept walking. Winston scratched his ear.

"At the restaurant . . ." Winston began.

Freddy's heart sank. He knew what was coming.

"Yeah?" Freddy swallowed hard.

"If you don't wanna talk about it you don't have to," Winston said quickly.

"No," Freddy took a deep breath, and let it out slowly. "You should know. When I was like, seventeen, I knew I was different. I wasn't ready to come out of the closet back then. You know, afraid of disappointing my family like it was a bad thing. So, I tried being straight. I pretended. Dated this girl who fell head over heels for me."

"Sounds familiar."

"Anyway, yeah. We dated and she kept wanting to be intimate. I couldn't put it off forever, so we had sex."

"That's no big deal. I mean, you were confused and repressed, which is awful, but having sex with a woman doesn't change you."

"She got pregnant."

"Oh."

"She loved me. I couldn't tell my parents, so I told Jennifer. She talked to the girl, explained to her the difficulty of being so young and pregnant, and Jen talked her into having an abortion."

"Shit."

"I was still just a dumb fucking kid. I knew how I felt about the girl, and I should have told her. I led her on, and then that happened. Jennifer bailed me out."

"It's fucked up she brought that out in the middle of the

restaurant."

"It is. But she's right. I am a fuck-up. I act without thinking about other people's emotions. I did it with you when I asked you to marry me. Everything about us feels so right, I didn't stop for one second to think about how *you* felt, and if I was going too fast."

Winston stopped suddenly. A twig snapped in the distance. Freddy's heart raced. He grabbed Winston's hand, squeezing it tight. Winston's palm was wet. Branches and palm fronds rustled, closer this time. Freddy held up the lantern like a shield while Winston pointed his flashlight like a sword. They shivered in the hot, humid air, breathing in unison as they waited for whatever it was to make its next move.

Freddy was taken down from behind. He dropped the lantern and the light went out. It happened so fast Winston barely had time to turn around before he, too, was knocked to the ground. The darkness was alive with the sound of grunting, squealing pigs.

Winston tried to get to his feet. The air was knocked out of his lungs and his arm was on fire. He wanted to look at it, but the grunting sound circled him. He looked for Freddy, shining his flashlight where he'd last seen him. Freddy lay on the ground, the lantern smashed into a thousand pieces against a small rock.

Winston pointed the flashlight wildly as the grunting grew closer. With a high-pitched squeal, he heard the pattering of hoofed feet charge from behind. He tried to get out of the way but was too slow. Winston felt the tusk embed itself in his side before his body was tossed into the air. His hand smacked the side of the animal. It felt like a sack of potatoes carpeted with steel wool.

"Winston!" Freddy shouted.

Winston hit the ground hard. He'd lost his flashlight. The darkness swallowed everything. He wasn't sure if he'd even opened his eyes. Then came a sound, a terrible shrill unlike any animal he'd ever heard. He saw the beam of the flashlight waving around like a lightsaber above him. Freddy cried out, and the pigs squealed in a way only a wounded animal could before stopping suddenly. The forest went silent. Not even the midnight insects dared make a sound.

Gingerly, Winston pulled himself up, nursing the wound in his side as he struggled to find balance. He found Freddy, standing frozen in the middle of the trail, the flashlight aimed at something blocking the path in front of them. Winston grabbed his shoulder to steady himself, looking at what the light was pointed at.

Three pigs lay dead in the middle of the trail, their necks broken. Two yellow eyes glowed farther down, flickering in the darkness like candles. In the narrow beam, all they could see was the faint silhouette of a flat nose and herpes-riddled lips. Their elevation gave the impression that this thing was taller than any man they'd ever seen.

Screams cried out in the distance back toward camp. It sounded like Jennifer. Freddy looked back for only a second, and when he aimed the light back toward the creature, it vanished.

16

AFTER EATING THE MAN, COOTER made her way back toward the Red Crab. There was a path running along a canal that was a straight shot all the way back to the restaurant. It was late in the afternoon, and the sun would go down soon. When she arrived, everyone was gone.

Cooter sniffed around, looking for Clive. His scent was everywhere, especially in the shed. She followed her nose, stepping back inside. There were small pools of scent littering the floor. It was a briny smell, something she'd only smelled when animals rotted.

She crawled under the table where he'd laid her a tarp as a sleeping area. She missed him, whimpering softly as she fell asleep. Car doors slammed closed, and an engine turned over. Cooter shot up in surprise, knocking over the worktable and showering the floor in mason jars and tools with a loud crash.

What should have taken at least fifteen minutes was finished in less than five. Jim panted over Abigail, dripping with sweat and shame as he unleaded his balls across his daughter's face.

"Jesus Christ, Pa!" Abigail hollered. "When was the last time you nutted?"

"Shut up!" Jim said, embarrassed. "Your Ma ain't been attentive to her duties none lately."

"You could have at least warned me!" Abigail wiped the warm, sticky cum from her eye.

"It just happens!" Pa explained. "You don't always have to say when shit happens."

"Ya coulda least aimed it outta my face!"

"All men aim for the face."

Abigail thought a moment, glad her brother was such a terrible shot.

"Now clean that shit off." Pa wiped his sweaty forehead. "I gotta finish that got-damn henhouse. That shit job your brother did couldn't keep in a chicken that was blind and deaf. Last time I leave that boy any job worth doin' right. Where did that motherfucker go? Fucker just makes my ass itch."

"He's 'round here somewhere, I suppose," Abigail said, trying not to laugh. After all, Clive *was* a motherfucker.

"Lazy ass," Pa grumbled, pulling up his pants and fastening his suspenders.

"Don't be hard on him. He's just soft."

"Soft as my limp dick."

"Ew!"

A noise rattled in the tool shed. The crash sounded like his work bench was knocked over

"Bastard better not be rubbing one out in my tool shed again." Pa stormed out of the Red Crab's men's room.

"Damn it, Pa!" Abigail said, her face still dripping with cum.

Abigail was helpless. With a thick wad of cum still in her eye, she couldn't see a damn thing. She knew she'd never make it in time.

Jim stomped his feet as he walked out of the kitchen and toward the shed. The city folk who'd been eating when he arrived were already gone. Any other time, not seeing their car in the driveway would have prompted him to make sure they'd paid, as he'd held up their only waitress in the bathroom. But Clive was up to his usual shit. Jim could smell it.

The shed door was wide-open, with much of its contents spilling out of the threshold.

"What the fuck?" Jim muttered to himself.

He stepped up to the open door, his body tense, waiting for anything that might happen next. Jim moved as quietly as possible so as not to spook whoever it was trespassing on his property. His mind ran through the possibilities. If it was Curious ol' Bob, he'd have smelled him all the way from the kitchen.

He knew it wasn't his son. If Clive ever had an idea, it'd have died of loneliness, but even he wasn't dumb enough to go messing with Jim's shed. Then Jim thought of the city folk. He imagined them in there, rummaging around for something shiny to steal.

Jim picked up a meat hook that'd fallen off the table. *Whoever it is*, he thought, *they'd better be ready for a fight.* The shed rocked and rattled as he heard a sound like a wild animal sniffing around inside.

As Jim placed his hand on the door, his foot stepped on a mason jar. It exploded, loud as a gunshot. The shed went quiet, and the sound went quiet. His heart pounded in his throat, sweat rained from his face, but still, Jim pulled open the shed door.

"Pa!" Abigail hollered. "Wait!"

It was too late. Jim opened the door. It happened too fast. He scarcely knew what was going on until it already finished. Something inside the shed lunged at him, knocking him over and onto the pile of broken glass. Jim felt the little shards dig into his hands and arms as he tried to catch himself. Dirt and debris was kicked up into his eyes as the thing trotted off toward Abigail.

Jim shouted as he rubbed his eyes with dusty, bloody hands and stammered toward where he last heard Abigail. With hook in hand, he swung violently, trying to catch whatever knocked him down. His eyes burned when he finally opened them. It was hazy, but he saw the outline of some grayish-colored hellhound with blue and red eyes. Jim gasped, then charged after it. The blurred creature moved faster than he'd expected. Jim, still shaken and off balance, fell over his own two feet.

"Stop it, Pa!" Abigail begged. "She ain't gonna hurt you!"

"Abigail!" Jim barked. "Get inside!"

"She's gone!" Abigail said, trying to grab the hook from her father.

"That's it!" Jim held the hook tight as a vice. "That's the thing that ate all our hens! We can't let it get away!"

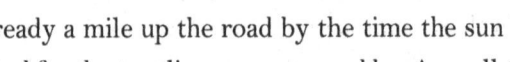

Cooter was already a mile up the road by the time the sun began to set. She darted for the tree line as a car raced by. A smell tickled her nose, spicy and sweet like tree sap. She followed it through the woods and into a clearing. Two people, a man and a woman, lay naked in front of a fire pit. The firelight was dim but bright enough for Cooter to see crude shadows and outlines of two knotted bodies across an air mattress.

The man pressed his hips into her from behind, grabbing fistfuls of hair as she twerked her ass in rhythm with his heavy thrusts. Cooter watched from the shadows, creeping up to them slowly as they changed position. The man rolled her on her back and buried his face between her legs. The woman arched her back, softly moaning as he lapped up their melded juices.

Cooter licked her lips as the man shuddered with excitement. He got up, biting the woman's melon-sized tits and suckling her nipples like a gleeful infant. Cooter stalked them silently, her body close to the ground. The man reared up suddenly, startling her.

The man looked in Cooter's direction as she ruffled the brush behind her. She ducked out of sight. The man shrugged, rubbed his wilting member back into life, and slid it back inside the woman. His grunting grew frantic, his breathing labored. The man curled his toes, pulling out his throbbing member in time to spray her face and large breasts with white-hot semen. He shouted as his body lurched from the icy hot tingling that surged through his body. The woman lay there, basking in his spray raining down on her like a shower.

Cooter could smell the man's seed perfume the air around her. Their stink of sex was beginning to have consequences on her own faculties. She felt her womb tighten as globs of vaginal secretions dripped from her labia. Cooter watched the man's throbbing penis bounce as it squeezed out every drop of its silk ooze.

Cooter made her approach, throwing all notions of stealth and discretion to the wind as her lustful desire took hold. The man heard her crawling noisily from the brush. One look, and he shouted in terror. The woman with him joined in a chorus of screams. Cooter made her move, lunging toward the man.

He was already on his feet and bolting toward the car, leaving the woman helpless on the ground. Cooter was fast, but not fast enough. The man was already in the car by the time she reached him, scratching and clawing the windows, purring and cooing for him to come to her. The man responded by turning the key and driving away.

"What the fuck?" shouted the woman. "Dean! *Chinga tu madre! Hijo de puto!*

Cooter turned toward the strange woman, still naked by the fire, covered in the man's seed.

"*Mierda*," she whispered to herself before running off into the forest.

Cooter reacted without thinking. Instinct took over as the prey began to run. It was a game, and she was winning.

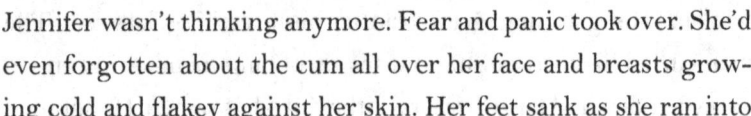

Jennifer wasn't thinking anymore. Fear and panic took over. She'd even forgotten about the cum all over her face and breasts growing cold and flakey against her skin. Her feet sank as she ran into a bog, her toes scraping against rocks and tree roots.

Jennifer looked behind her, and the creature was almost on top of her. In the darkness, she couldn't see the brush she'd run into, it was all sawgrass and cattails. The long, serrated leaves slashed her naked skin. Jennifer cried out as she felt her body being torn to shreds. She remembered a show on television about the worst ways to die. Among them was death by a thousand cuts. She now understood why.

The sawgrass cut deeply across her arms, legs, and sides. One of them slid across her nipple, slicing it almost in half. Jennifer stopped, falling to her knees and shouting as the pain grew unbearable. She looked behind her, wailing with tears as she cupped her aching breast. The thing was gone. It didn't dare chase after her through the sawgrass. Ahead of her, she could see a clearing. She was almost there, almost home free.

Jennifer mustered all her strength and dragged herself the last few feet out of the grass. On the other side she found solid ground and collapsed on the riverbank, sobbing. Her body was torn to ribbons, and she felt blood dripping from everywhere, but at least she was safe. She covered her eyes, wishing it was all just a dream.

Dean left her to die. What about Freddy? Or Winston? They'd

not come back yet. If the monster went back to the camp, they'd be walking right into the monster's clutches.

A sound grumbled nearby. Jennifer uncovered her face. Blue and red eyes stared back at her. Jennifer screamed as the creature ran its sandpaper-like tongue across her body. Its saliva stung at first, then left a trail of numbness across everything it touched. Jennifer felt violated but knew it would soon be over.

The monster lunged, biting down hard on her breasts. She could feel its three long fangs dig into her silicone implant and the strange draining sensation as it lapped up the viscous fluid inside. The creature gagged at the terrible taste before spitting out the silicone and dragging its tongue along the dirt.

The pain was excruciating, but meant survival. The creature's saliva numbed Jennifer just enough for her to come to her senses. Grabbing her sagging breast, Jennifer got to her feet and ran. This time, the creature did not follow. Whatever it was, it lost its appetite.

17

DEAN SPED DOWN THE ROAD as quickly as the SUV could take him. His heart was still racing, as was his mind, as he tried to comprehend what the hell he'd just seen. Not once did he think about Jennifer, Winston, or Freddy. This trip was ruined, and it was all their fault. It was only then that he even realized he was still naked. He laughed, shaking his head.

After setting the cruise control, Dean sighed with relief, relaxing in his seat. A massive hand shot through his windshield and turned the steering wheel, flipping the vehicle in the process. It happened so fast, like a gunshot, Dean barely had time to scream as the vehicle tumbled like a log down the road.

By the time the SUV settled into a ditch by the road, Dean found himself upside down with a face full of broken glass. His vision blurred in and out of focus. A stink like burning tires and ammonia filled the air. It was a wretched smell, like a skunk he'd found out back when he was a kid. The memory made him think of his life flashing before his eyes, but the smell kept him conscious.

Metal buckled and twisted as the door was ripped from its

hinges. Dean could barely see the massive hands yank him out of the seatbelt like a ripe orange from a tree. The rough palms scratched against his soft naked flesh. As things came into focus, Dean found himself staring into the eyes of the massive skunk ape.

Its yellow eyes studied him before pressing its nose against his skin, deeply breathing him in. Dean cried, bawling like a child as his bladder released its contents. The skunk ape jerked in surprise, then cupped its hand under the gentle stream and sampled some of Dean's golden water. He looked at the creature's terrible features. Its face was littered with warts and cold sores. It licked its coarse lips and grimaced.

Dean felt something tap the souls of his feet. He looked down and saw the creature sporting a stiff red rocket. The tip of its penis was long and thin like a dog, poking out just behind its tight foreskin. Dean wept.

The skunk ape lifted him higher in the air, sniffing his crotch. It poked out its tongue and tasted the dried, sticky juices along the shaft of Dean's penis and ball sack. Its tongue was rough and lumpy with a thick slimy film that smelled like butter above the skunk odor. The tickling sensation disturbed him as his body reacted instinctively with a stiff boner.

"Bro!" he whimpered. "Please! No! Please, God, no!"

The skunk ape patted Dean on the head. It drooled a thin bead of saliva over its cock and brought Dean down on top of it. The drool aided little, as the skunk ape's cock was the girth of Dean's arm. He cried out as he felt the tip pierce his tightly pinched sphincter. Harder, the skunk ape pressed Dean over its cock, indifferent to his cries and thrashing as it closed its eyes with the satisfaction of stepping into a hot bath.

Dean felt the skin around his ass stretch to its tearing point. He gasped as the tip slipped the rest of the way in. The pain was like being fisted by some enormous hand. It was a strange juxta-position of agony and pleasure as the skunk ape's rough and warty cock scraped against his prostate. Dean's balls throbbed, and his own penis stiffened to the point of agony. He wanted it to be over. He wanted to wake up from this terrible nightmare, but the skunk ape had only just begun.

It moaned passionately, grunting and huffing its hot gingivitis breath in Dean's face. He could feel the lumpy, herpes-riddled shaft force its way deeper into his colon. He felt the massive cock in his stomach as blood melded with the shit and pre-cum in his anus.

The creature lifted Dean, then pushed him down again, sliding him up and down its shaft like a Fleshlight. Its body quivered with tantalizing pleasure while Dean cried out helplessly. The skunk ape's cock throbbed on the edge of climax, but it did not pull out. It forced itself deeper inside Dean until his ass cheeks rested against its pelvis, and the skunk ape unloaded inside him.

Cum jetted by the bucket load as it fired off four hot streams somewhere in his small intestine. Dean shuttered at the strange and terrible sensation, his eyes too dry to cry. With the care of a discarded condom, the skunk ape slid Dean off its wilted member and tossed him back into the ditch.

Dean landed like a rag doll, his body folded in the downward dog position. His ass was hot and wet, oozing with creamy pink-ish-brown fluids. Dean felt nothing as his mind carried him off to a safer place, one that could only be found in unconsciousness.

18

JENNIFER LIMPED HER WAY BACK to camp. Her legs ached, and her throat and lungs burned from all her screaming. Sweat dripped down her body and into her cuts, stinging her every step of the way. By the time she made it back, she was exhausted.

All her clean clothes were still in the back of the SUV. Dean abandoned not just her, but Freddy and Winston. Jennifer picked through the clothes she'd worn before they had sex. In the heat of the moment, they'd thrown them off with little regard to where they landed. Her clothes were caked in dirt and mud. Normally, she'd have been mortified at even the thought of wearing these filthy rags, but anything was better than running naked like that again.

It wasn't until Jennifer slid on her panties and bra that she noticed the bug bites. The adrenaline rush and painful cuts numbed her to the mosquitoes feasting on her flesh. Seeing them for the first time sent itching, tingling sensations throughout her body. It took everything in her not to scratch and claw her skin.

Dressing was miserable work. Jennifer's clothes were gritty

and sandy while her skin itched and burned. She felt violated by filth as it crept in every nook and cranny, in every intimate and sacred place on her body. Blood quickly soaked into the soiled fabric. The sight of so much blood made her woozy. She sat down on the air mattress she'd shared with Dean. It still smelled like sex.

The campfire was almost out, with only a few coals glowing in the ash. She slid in a few logs they'd laid out beside the fire to dry. One caught fire, while the other sizzled like steak. It wasn't much light, but it was better than nothing.

Jennifer couldn't help but think of her brother. Then she remembered Dean's phone. Last time she'd seen it, he'd slid it back in his pocket. He'd left in a panic, still naked as he drove off.

Jennifer dove for his clothes and checked all his pockets. She found it and thought a moment, trying to remember Dean's password. She forgot the emergency call button, and typed in the numbers, and the phone buzzed Incorrect. Frantically, she tried again, with the same results. Jennifer grunted, then stopped, taking a few deep breaths to clear her head. She tried the only other password she could think of, 'Protein.' The home screen opened.

"Oh God!" she cheered and called her brother's phone.

Voicemail. Jennifer tried again—no ringing, no dial tone, just straight to voicemail. She looked at the home screen. There was full reception, but only one percent battery left. She dialed 911.

The phone rang.

"911 emergency," the operator said on the other line.

"My boyfriend and I were attacked by an animal!" Jennifer didn't notice how frantic she sounded until the woman on the other end replied.

"It's okay," the operator replied. "Where are you now?"

"I don't know." Panic stole the last bit of breath left from her lungs, and her voice shook as she spoke. "Dean never told me the name of the park."

"I can look up your GPS," the operator assured her. "We will send help. Is anyone inj—"

The phone cut off as the battery died.

"No!" Jennifer whispered. "No! Please! God, please! No!"

She pressed the power button, but the phone was dead. With her last ounce of energy, she screamed at the plastic box before throwing it out into the forest.

"What the fuck?" Freddy shouted.

"*Niño!*" Jennifer cheered.

Jennifer rushed to her feet and ran toward him. She went to hug him, but saw Winston propped up over his arms.

"We have to get him to the hospital," Freddy said. "Where's Dean?"

"*Puto* left us!" Jennifer helped carry Winston.

"He did what?" Freddy yelled. "What the fuck happened?"

"Something came from the woods. A wild animal. It attacked us. Dean left me to die!"

"Son of a bitch!"

"Winston needs to rest. Put him on the air mattress."

They carried Winston over to the mattress and carefully laid him down.

"Is your phone on?" Jennifer asked Freddy.

"I've got no reception out here," he replied.

"Dean's phone is dead," she said before gasping at the sight of Winston's wounds. "*Celindo*, what happened?"

"Wild pigs," Freddy said.

"*Pobrecito,*" Jennifer rubbed the back of her hand against Winston's cheek. "We'll get you home."

"What happened to you?" Freddy asked as he saw Jennifer better in the light. "What the hell is going on here?"

"The animal chased me into the swamp. But I got lost and went through the sawgrass. It cut me bad."

"Are you okay? What did it look like?"

"I'm hurt, but okay, I guess. The animal? It was big, like a dog. But it had no hair, and its eyes were red and blue."

"What the fuck?"

"It was scary, *mijo*. I thought I was going to die."

"Something else happened to us in the woods. Something saved us, but I'm not sure that's what it wanted."

"What do you mean?"

"Something killed the pigs. Like, it snapped their necks! I don't think it wanted to rescue us, though. I think it wanted us for itself. It smelled real bad, too. Like a skunk or something."

"What the fuck is going on? I found Dean's phone and tried to call you. But it went to voicemail. I called the police, but the battery died. I don't know if they heard me!"

"We'll get out of this! We just have to keep our heads straight."

"What do we do? I don't want to die . . . why the fuck did he leave me?"

"Calm down! You're my sister. I'm not going to leave you! All right? I promise."

"Excuse me?" a man asked from the shadows.

"Who the fuck are you?" Freddy shot up to his feet.

"Sorry," the man said, raising his hands to show he meant no harm. "Name's Clive."

"You're that guy from the restaurant," Freddy said.

"Well," Clive shrugged. "Yeah, Pa owns it. My sister and I work around there."

"Please," Jennifer pleaded. "We need help. Our friend is hurt."

"I'm sorry ma'am,'" Clive sighed. "I'm just passing through. I'm looking for my dog."

"Didn't you hear her?" Freddy shouted. "We need help! Something attacked us!"

"Oh no," Clive said with genuine concern. "What did it look like?"

"What does it matter?" Freddy asked. "We need to get the fuck out of here!"

"I won't ask again," Clive said, exposing the butt of the rifle to show them he meant business. "What did it look like?"

"It was two different animals," Freddy said. "First, we were jumped by some wild pigs, then something saved us. Something bad. It snapped their necks, all of them! It was big, and it smelled like a skunk."

"Curious ol' Bob." Clive shivered. "If he's out here, it don't mean no good for nobody."

"I was attacked by some wolf," Jennifer tried to explain. "But it looked like a bear. I don't know what it was. It had no hair and evil eyes."

"Cooter!" Clive hooted. "My baby girl! Where did she go?"

"Your fucking dog attacked me!" Jennifer shouted. "It bit me in the fucking tit!"

"I swear," Clive defended, "Cooter don't mean no harm. She's just a wild animal. You gotta treat 'em right, and show 'em who's boss is all. You act scared around a wild animal, they think you's prey, and they hunt you down as such."

"We're wasting time!" Freddy shouted. "Winston is dying!"

"And I gotta find my dog before Curious ol' Bob does!" Clive grabbed for his gun. "Or even worse, before Pa does!"

Jennifer looked on the ground for anything she could use to defend herself. Her shoe sat inches from her feet. She looked up at Clive, whose attention was fixed on her brother. Slowly, she knelt down and grabbed it, and with all the strength she had left,

Jennifer made her attack.

In one swift motion, Clive was on the ground while Jennifer pummeled him with her shoe, spitting curses both in Spanish and English.

"Holy shit!" Freddy gasped.

"I'm sorry!" Clive finally submitted.

"Never underestimate the power of the *chancla*!" Jennifer said, yanking the rifle from his arm.

19

JIM QUICKLY GAVE UP CHASING the thing on foot. Running into the glades unarmed was suicide, especially when he knew Curious ol' Bob was nearing the rutting season. He went back to the house and armed himself to the teeth. Jim didn't just grab his rifle. He grabbed his machete, Colt .45, a stumpy .45 Magnum revolver, short stock AK-47, and his Remington shotgun with bear slugs and enough ammunition to supply a small militia. He wasn't sure what he'd run into, but he was ready for anything. Abigail stormed off somewhere, no doubt to tell her Ma what was happening. Jim didn't have much time.

Sitting in his truck, Jim thought a moment. The thing could be anywhere. He needed to get help. He had to get the other families involved. Diabetus Dave was the closest, and his kids were damn good shots. He hopped in his truck and raced over.

Police were all over Diabetus Dave's property. A grim feeling sank to the bottom of his belly at the sight of so many lawmen. He got out of his truck and walked toward Billy, Dave's youngest, balled up on the porch.

"What happened?" Jim asked. "Where's ya daddy? Where's ya

ma?"

"Daddy . . ." Billy sniffled, his face and eyes red from bawling. "Daddy's dead!"

"No!" Jim gasped.

"Something from the woods came. Daddy heard it spook the goats and went out to get it, but it killed him."

"Where's ya ma and ya brothers?"

"Inside talking to the police. Shamus is at work, and John's inside consoling Mama. I can't see her like that. I miss my daddy."

Jim knelt beside the boy.

"I promise," Jim said in a calm, steady voice as he placed his hand on his shoulder. "I'll find that monster that done killed ya daddy. I will hunt that cocksucker down, and when I find it, may God have mercy on its soul."

Jim hopped back in his truck and sped off down the road. His blood boiled. Then he remembered those city folk at the restaurant. Abigail said something about them camping out in the glades. They were in danger. There were only a few places open for camping this time of year and Jim knew exactly where they'd be. He only hoped he'd make it in time.

Night already fell by the time he came across the car accident. Jim slowed down after he recognized the SUV. It was the one from the restaurant. He pulled over and hopped out of the car. His shotgun was cocked and ready and his AK-47 was strapped to his back. The young man on the grass was not well. His face was planted in the dirt, and his naked ass pointed toward the heavens, gaping and oozing with shit, blood, and semen. His whole body was white as a ghost. Jim was too late.

"Mother of God," he exclaimed as the stink of skunk ape flared up in his nostrils. "Shit! That'll gag a maggot! Boy, you all right?"

The kid didn't answer, only grunted in agony and exhaustion.

"Of course ya ain't." Jim shook his head and knelt down beside him. "Looks like Curious ol' Bob's been rompin' around your innards. Don't s'pose you could walk in the state ya in. C'mon boy, we'll get you back in my truck."

Jim slung the shotgun around his shoulder and gingerly picked up the naked kid. He was lighter than he'd expected, guessing most of the boy's fluids were spilled across the grass by now. Gently, he laid the kid out in the truck bed and covered him with the blue tarp.

"Sorry to see ya like this," Jim shook his head. "What happened to the rest of 'em?"

"The thing . . ." the kid said with a trembling voice. "The animal, it came from the swamp. It chased me. It wanted to kill me. But I got in the car. I thought I was safe, but then that monster got me. He . . . he . . . oh God! My ass! It fucked my ass!"

"Sure did," Jim frowned. "You'll wanna get yourself checked out. See, we call him Curious ol' Bob because the skunk ape is bi-curious. If it moves, he'll fuck it. If it's dead, well . . . he'll fuck it anyway. Back a few years ago, we had these monkeys escape from some science lab in Miami.

"Them things was infected with herpes. If you saw Curious ol' Bob's face, you know where this story is going. When you get back in town, you might wanna get a doctor to check you out. Where's ya camp?"

Dean told Jim as best he could. Jim knew the campground well enough and sped on toward it.

←——————————————→

Jennifer pointed her shoe at Clive, lying on the ground. She handed his weapon to Freddy, who held it carefully to his shoulder.

"Sorry," Freddy chuckled. "Never fuck with an angry Latina."

"You don't understand!" Clive cried. "Cooter's my only friend in the world. She don't mean nothin'! She's just like any other animal. You gotta believe that! She don't mean to hurt nobody, I swear!"

"Shut up *puto!*" Jennifer shouted. "I'm sick and tired of all this bullshit! I want to go home. You will show us out of this fucking swamp and help us get our friend to the fucking hospital. Do you understand?"

Before Clive could answer, a smell drifted over the air. It was a dank, musty odor that stank like burnt tires. Clive wet himself.

"We're fucked," he said under his breath.

Something moved in the shadows. Freddy tried to follow it with the rifle, but it was too quick. He'd never held a gun before, and the long weapon felt unwieldy in his arms. The light of the campfire was fading as the wet log spat water and sap over the dying coals. The shadows encroached as the sound of branches breaking and leaves rustling moved around them with incredible speed.

A massive hand reached from the forest for Winston. Freddy turned just in time, as the fingers caressed his tired face. He smacked the knuckles with the butt of his rifle. The creature grunted from the shadows and withdrew its hand before scurrying off into the brush. It reached from the darkness toward Jennifer, who swatted it back with her shoe. Again, the hand withdrew, and the creature skulked in the shadows.

Limbs snapped like firecrackers as a tree fell toward them. Jennifer and Freddy barely leapt out of the way, but Clive was too slow. The old pine landed right on his ankle, crushing it under its weight. Clive shouted in pain as he tried to yank himself free. The rough bark scratched him deep as he managed to free himself. His foot was twisted at a ninety-degree angle in the wrong direction, with bits of bone sticking out through splintered skin.

"Mother fuck!" Clive cried out, grabbing the wound and hurting himself further.

Jennifer ran to his side, trying her best to drag him away. With the last of the campfire still burning, Curious ol' Bob stepped out of the woods. He was a brute, over eight feet tall, with the face and body of an orangutan, walking upright like a man. His fur was a rat's nest of reddish brown dreadlocks and he stank to high heaven. Jennifer choked as she tried not to vomit on Clive.

"Shoot it!" Jennifer gagged.

Freddy forgot he was holding the rifle. He pointed the gun and squeezed the trigger. The gun recoiled and cracked his shoulder. Freddy yelled at the pain as he felt his joint dislocate. His shot missed, exploding in the tree behind Curious ol' Bob. Freddy gritted his teeth and brought the rifle to his shoulder again and squeezed the trigger. Nothing happened.

"You gotta cock it, fuckhead!" Clive hollered.

Freddy looked at the bolt action. He might have been staring at the workings of an internal combustion engine. Remembering all the years of video games and television, Freddy tried to replicate what he saw on the movies. He didn't expected the lever to be so difficult to slide in and out of place, and with his shoulder screaming in pain, it was even harder to find leverage.

Curious ol' Bob was right on top of him. Freddy abandoned trying to cock the weapon and swung it like a club. The pain in his arm was excruciating, slowing his swing. Curious ol' Bob grabbed it midair and snatched it from his hands. Freddy backed away as it dropped the weapon on the ground. It licked its herpes-riddled lips as its cock grew stiff between its legs.

Freddy tried to turn and run, but Curious ol' Bob grabbed him by the back of his neck and lifted him into the air. He could feel the tip of its cock smacking the souls of his shoes. Jennifer looked around her, trying to find anything she could use as a weapon. She saw the riffle sitting in the dirt behind the skunk ape, too far. She looked closer around her. The wet log. The end that was in the fire finally ignited while the other end spat more sap and moisture. She slipped her shoe back on, grabbed the log, and ran toward her brother.

Curious ol' Bob massaged Freddy's salty, teary cheek with its hot and slimy tongue. With all her might, Jennifer swung the burning end of the log right into Curious ol' Bob's nut sack. The creature gasped, releasing its grip as burning embers exploded against its scrotum. Freddy landed hard as Jennifer helped him to his feet. Curious ol' Bob scowled, shaking off the pain as it ran back into the brush.

"Where'd he go?" Freddy asked.

"We're all gonna die!" Clive shouted.

"Shut the fuck up!" Jennifer yelled back. "We gotta move!"

Curious ol' Bob ran with astonishing speed, leaping through the forest like a spider monkey. The fire was spent as the last of the coals burned out. The camp was engulfed in darkness. Jennifer was yanked from her brother's side. He could hear her screams fade as she was tossed into the air.

"Jen!" Freddy called out.

Something struck him from behind. Freddy fell hard, biting the inside of his lip as his jaw smacked the ground. He could taste the blood as his chest went numb from the impact. Curious ol' Bob's fingers explored the brim of his pants. With one swift move, they were ripped open around his ass while it slid his shirt up to his shoulders. Freddy tried to crawl away, but Curious ol' Bob held him firm. Globs of hot pre-cum dripped onto his back like hot wax, sending terrible goosebumps up his spine.

A gunshot sounded with a flash of muzzle fire. Curious ol' Bob released him and shot upwards as the bullet struck his side. Clive cocked his rifle and took aim again. Curious ol' Bob was too fast. In an instant, it jumped back into the brush. The dim light of the moon did little under the dense forest. Clive couldn't get a bead on him. Then he saw them, the two great yellow eyes staring down from above.

Before Clive could get another shot, Curious ol' Bob snatched the gun and broke it over his knee. Wood and metal splintered in the air as Clive tried to shield his face as best he could. As Curious ol' Bob went to make his final attack, something shrieked from the shadows.

Cooter lunged from the forest and onto Curious ol' Bob's shoulders. She scratched and clawed the skunk ape, her nails barely long enough to cut through his dense fur.

"Cooter!" Clive hollered. "Save yourself!"

Cooter ignored him and bit down on Curious ol' Bob's neck. He grumbled and roared before yanking her off. She fought, swinging her claws and snapping her jaws wildly. Curious ol' Bob roared in her face with his putrid breath and slammed her into the ground.

"No!" Clive shouted. "You fucker! I'm gonna kill you!"

Curious ol' Bob looked at his cock. It wilted like old asparagus. He grumbled as he toyed with it, trying to bring it back to life. Cooter coughed, trying to get herself back to her feet. Curious ol' Bob raised both fists in the air, ready to bring them down hard. It stopped short as a shoe struck him in the face.

"*Chupame la verga!*" Jennifer said, holding her other shoe in her hand.

Truck lights flashed from the forest onto Curious ol' Bob's face, momentarily blinding him. Jim fired his shotgun. It clapped like thunder through the forest as the slug collided with Curious ol' Bob's shoulder. In the time it'd taken Jim to cock the shotgun and aim, the skunk ape vanished. Silence fell as Jim scanned he tree line. Something yanked him by his foot and lifted him into the air. Curious ol' Bob snatched him by the leg and thrashed him repeatedly into the ground.

Jim's body cracked and popped under the punishment. His face was broken into an unrecognizable mess and ribs pierced through his skin. Curious ol' Bob dropped him and licked his open wounds. Jim could feel the rough, slimy tongue like a snail exploring the meat of his cheeks and exposed teeth as it dragged along his face.

Clive watched as the skunk ape readied to defile his father right next to him. Then he caught sight of the AK-47 still looped around his pa's neck. If he could just reach it, he might stand a chance.

Curious ol' Bob rested his bruised ball sack against Jim's face while he ripped off his suspenders. It hurt to breathe, and the stink of skunk ape scrotum made his suffering even worse. Curious ol' Bob stood up and prepared to mount him. As he began to spread Jim's cheeks, something attacked him from behind.

Cooter bit down with all her might on the skunk ape's nuts. Curious ol' Bob shrilled in a high voice like nails on a chalkboard. Cooter's grip was relentless, even as the skunk ape slammed her around. She dug her claws into the thin flesh around his taint and yanked his balls with all her might. His skin began to tear as blood sprayed her face and nose until his balls were ripped completely off.

Curious ol' Bob roared in agony, grabbing the dripping wound as he stormed off into the glades. Cooter plopped his testicles on the ground like two fleshy oranges and howled triumphantly at the moon.

20

"COOTER!" CLIVE SMILED. "YA WONDERFUL bastard, get over here!"

Cooter panted and limped over. She licked Clive's face as he hugged and kissed her. A gunshot fired from the truck and a bullet slammed into her back leg. Cooter yelped as she fell to the ground.

"No!" Clive cried.

Dean pulled back the hammer on the .45 revolver, pointing it at Cooter.

"Stop!" Freddy shouted as he jumped in front of Cooter.

"What the fuck is wrong with you?" Jennifer yelled. "This thing just saved our lives!"

"Don't you see?" Dean whimpered. "This thing ruined everything!"

"What the fuck are you talking about?" Freddy asked.

"Bro, I planned this shit out for years!" Dean coughed, trying to hold the gun steady. "I used every penny I had on this trip. From the plane, to the rental, to the fucking engagement ring!"

"What fucking engagement ring?" Jennifer glared.

"Yeah," Dean shook his head. "I was gonna propose to your

ass. Then your brother here fucked it up right from the beginning. This fucking loser can't keep his dick in his pants!"

"You left me to die!" Jennifer pointed at Cooter. "Before we knew what the hell was going on, when that thing came into camp, you ditched me!"

"What the hell was I supposed to do?" Dean cried. "I wasn't gonna die for you. You chose that loser over me the second you invited him on this trip. I told you back home this was just us, just you and me, but no! You had to drag his cheating ass along for the ride. I've had enough. And if you won't get the hell out of my way, then this bullet's for you, too."

Another shot rang out, but it wasn't from Dean. A hole the size of a coaster exploded in the middle of his chest. Everyone gasped. Winston cocked Jim's shotgun and spat on the ground.

"No one fucks with my fiancé," he said before throwing the weapon onto the ground.

Freddy ran to Winston and grabbed him before he collapsed.

"I told you the black guy always dies," Winston smiled.

"No!" Freddy said. "You said the black guy dies first. I think the white guy beat ya to it. Stay with me, we'll get help."

Police sirens sounded in the distance.

"Oh shit." Jennifer looked at Cooter.

"What?" Clive asked, rubbing Cooter's back.

"If there's police coming," Jennifer explained, "then Cooter can't be here. They'll take her away, lock her in a shelter or a zoo."

Cooter shivered, as if she understood what Jennifer was saying.

"Wait," Clive looked her over. "You understand every word we're saying?"

Cooter nodded.

"Now, I ain't gonna ask how," Clive continued, "'cause that don't matter none. What does matter is that I don't want nothin' happenin' to you. I love you, Cooter. That's the God's truth. Ain't ever had a pup like you! Well, never had a pup at all. Never will, I s'pose, 'cause their ain't no replacin' you."

Cooter licked Clive's face and frowned.

"Hurry up," Jennifer ordered as the sirens drew closer.

"She's right, ya know," Clive sniffled. "Them lawman are gonna be all over now that the murders are everywhere. I dunno what happened with Diabetus Dave, but I forgive you. I trust you didn't do it in spite. You're still just a wild animal. I need to remind myself that from time to time.

"Now you go on and get. I can't keep you from being yourself. You gotta go be free. Be free for the both of us, will you?"

Cooter bowed her head and rubbed her maw against Clive's cheek. She purred like an asthmatic cat and licked his face one last time. Cooter got to her feet and trotted off back into the Everglades. Clive held back the tears the best he could.

The police came like a swarm of mosquitoes buzzing with questions. They asked about Jim and Dean, and about the animal Jennifer reported.

"It must have been a bear," she told one officer, watching as they wheeled Winston away on a gurney.

"Maybe," the officer replied, looking at Jim's broken body. "I've never seen any animal do damage like that."

"Definitely a bear," she replied.

"He's coming with," Winston said to one of the EMTs stopping Freddy from getting in the ambulance with him. "He's a d-bag, but he's my fiancé."

"I like how that sounds," Freddy smiled before kissing Winston.

"Smells like a skunk went to town over here," another EMT said, helping Clive onto a gurney.

"You got that right," Clive said, never once looking away from where he'd last seen Cooter. "Somethin' sure as hell did."

At the hospital, Abigail and Clive's mother, Margay, came to visit. Abigail brought a vase of flowers, and Margay brought some fresh frog legs she'd fried up just for him. His mother was a rotund woman who sidestepped to get inside the room. All her clothes were made from scraps she'd gotten at the thrift store. Curtains mostly, all knitted into strange and askew patterns that only she could appreciate.

"Have you heard about Pa?" Clive asked. "They haven't told me nothin' yet."

"He's gonna make it," Abigail said. "He's in surgery. Doctors say he won't be pretty, but he'll be okay."

"I made these just for you," Margay laid the Styrofoam container on the bed tray beside him. "I'm just glad you're all right. I'm so proud of you."

"Motherfucker." Abigail smiled.

"Watch that mouth!" Margay scolded. "I heard from the gay boy what you did. He told me all about Curious ol' Bob."

"He tell you about Cooter?" Clive asked shamefully.

"No. Abigail did. Right after Pa went huntin' after her. I swear, sometimes he's got about as much sense as God gave an ant. Once his temper gets the best of him, there ain't no stopping all that stupid. It's a shame what happened to Curious ol' Bob."

"What is?" Clive asked, surprised.

"Well," Margay blushed, "let's just say, once you get past the smell, Curious ol' Bob ain't half bad."

Acknowledgments

Special thanks to Melanie O'Brien, Garret Cook, Gillian, Megan, Zane, Meagan, Victoria, Victoria, Victoria (y'all know who you are!), Jim Coniglio, Chuck Buda, Armand Rosamilia, Mr. Frank, Scott Groverston, Tommy Clark, and the rest of the Necrocasticon Podcast. Without your support, and your putting up with me talking about this fucked up little story, it might never have happened!

Bio

Lucas Milliron resides in his home in South Florida. He's the oldest of three siblings and the first of his family's history to graduate high school and college. Lucas is an author of quiet, extreme, and fantastical fiction.

LucasMilliron.com
Facebook - facebook.com/lucasldo
Instagram - @MillironLucas
Twitter - @BeardedOptician

Other Grindhouse Press Titles